Knives and Nuptials

Wendy the Wedding Planner Cozy Mystery

Cindy B

ISBN-13: 978-1505257595

ISBN-10: 150525759X

More Cozy Mysteries by Cindy Bell

Dune House Cozy Mystery Series

Seaside Secrets

Heavenly Highland Inn Cozy Mystery Series

Murdering the Roses

Dead in the Daisies

Killing the Carnations

Drowning the Daffodils

Suffocating the Sunflowers

Bekki the Beautician Cozy Mystery Series

Table of Contents

Chapter One

Words were blurring on the page in front of Wendy. She was trying to push herself to stay awake for an extra hour so that she could review the progress of Anne Max's wedding plans. She had been so busy lately that she was trying to fit more hours into the day. As joyful as it was to be part of a person's special day, it could also be very nerve wracking. Wendy liked everything to be perfect, she liked to make sure that the bride and groom had a day that they could treasure for the rest of their lives. However, at some point table settings and china patterns began to fade into each other creating quite an interesting kaleidoscope every time she closed her eyes.

"All right," she yawned and snapped her large planner shut. It was nearly bursting at the seams with samples and sticky notes. It was a far cry from the modern version, a nearly paper thin tablet that could store the universe in tiny little apps. But Wendy liked having the real thing in front of her. She had her tablet, too, but it was what she used when meeting with clients. There was something soothing about the patchwork style of a stuffed binder. As she carried it inside from her small patio, she felt her sleepiness growing. She locked the patio door behind her, dropped the binder on her desk, and then collapsed into bed.

Wendy was becoming fonder of her condo since she no longer had to share it with her ex-boyfriend. She was remembering what it was like to have real privacy. It was amazing to think how different her life had been not too long ago. She had been preparing to marry a man she didn't even realize she didn't love, until he had walked out on her. She had been employed by a very prestigious wedding planner, until she had met an unfortunate end. Now, Wendy had her privacy once more, she had her own business as a wedding planner, and she had a new love interest.

"Brian," she murmured to herself as she sprawled out on her bed. Brian had come into her life exactly when she had needed him. He was a private investigator who had helped her out of a very dicey situation. Ever since, he had been a constant presence in her mind, and heart. Their relationship was tentative at best, with barely a kiss between them, but it was more powerful than she had ever experienced before.

Wendy, who was surrounded every day all day by blushing brides and hopeful grooms, was a romantic at heart. She loved the idea of love. She loved it so much, that she had almost conned herself into believing she was in love with her ex. It wasn't until she had looked into Brian's eyes that she had realized that love isn't something that can be found between the pages of a book, or in a certain pattern, or even in the rhythm of a ballad. In fact, in her current opinion, it wasn't something that could be found at all. It was something that had to find her. She hugged her pillow and curled up on her bed as she smiled. She was fairly certain, that this time, it had actually found her. Did Brian feel the same way? She fell asleep wondering if she would ever know the answer to that question.

***

After what felt like only a few moments of slumber, Wendy woke to her phone chiming first thing in the morning. It was actually too early for it be her alarm. She picked up the phone and looked at the caller ID. Anne Max flashed on the screen.

"Hello?" she mumbled and cleared her throat as she answered the phone.

"Hello? Wendy?" Anne said quickly. "I'm sorry to call so early," she said in a sweet, apologetic tone. "It's just, I was wondering if you could join me this morning. I'm doing the final fitting for my dress, and I'd love to have your opinion on it."

"That's fine," Wendy assured her in a bright tone. "I'd love to see you in your dress."

There were many things that Wendy took care of before wedding crunch time, and many things that most brides wanted to do personally. Wendy had her own selection of vendors for the weddings, such as florists, decorators, and caterers that she relied on because of past experience with them. Anne had a dress she had been dreaming of wearing, and had no question about what she wanted. It wasn't something that Wendy had to help her choose. As a result Wendy hadn't had the chance to see the dress except in photographs.

"Can we meet up at Barney's Bridal around nine?" Anne requested.

"Absolutely, I'll be there," Wendy replied warmly before hanging up the phone. She hugged her pillow a moment longer. Then her phone chimed again. She picked it up, expecting it be Anne again.

"Hello?" she asked in a rushed voice.

"Good morning," Brian replied perkily.

Wendy blushed immediately. She shoved her pillow away and sat up. "Oh Brian, I didn't know it was you," she said quickly.

"Disappointed?" he asked with a slight chuckle.

"Not at all, I was up half the night thinking about you," Wendy rushed to say, and then immediately felt foolish. She wondered how she was going to get out of this one.

"Really?" Brian asked with interest. "Just what were you thinking about?"

"I meant the wedding, I was thinking about the wedding," Wendy stammered out.

"Our wedding?" he asked with surprise.

"What?" Wendy blinked and then gulped. "What do you mean our wedding?"

"I don't know, you're the one that brought it up," Brian pointed out with a laugh. She could tell that he was getting pleasure from all of her squirming.

"Brian, stop!" Wendy laughed. "What I meant to say was that I was up half of the night working on Anne Max's wedding, and yes, I thought about you as well, which means I was not the least bit disappointed when it turned out to be you on the phone."

"Well, now that we have that all cleared up," Brian murmured. "Maybe we could meet for breakfast?"

"Oh, I can't," Wendy sighed. "I just promised to meet Anne this morning to see her wedding dress."

"All right," Brian agreed with some

disappointment. "Whenever you're free, just let me know. I'd love to see you."

"I will let you know," Wendy promised him.

"I'm glad to see that your business is doing so well," Brian added.

"And yours?" Wendy asked as she climbed out of bed. "Are you hunting cats or are you stalking husbands?"

"Maybe a little of both?" Brian suggested.

"Well, whatever you are doing, please be careful," Wendy said warmly.

"Always," he replied. "See you soon, Wendy."

"See you soon, Brian," Wendy replied and hung up the phone. She held the phone between her cheek and shoulder as she sighed dreamily. Only then did she realize she hadn't actually hung up the phone. "Oops," she nearly dropped the phone as she fumbled with it to turn it off.

Wendy took a quick shower. Then she did her best to tame her ear-length strawberry blonde curls. They never seemed to want to cooperate with her. She enhanced her deep green eyes with a hint of mascara, and added a few light strokes of blush to disguise her pale skin. Her grandmother had once called it porcelain. Wendy called it pasty.

***

As Wendy drove along the promenade she saw the usual happy sights. The beach was dotted with joggers, runners, and wanderers. Wendy was usually one of them but she hadn't been able to get up early enough for her walk that morning. The town was busy but quaint with several tourist traps nestled amidst local small businesses. There were not too many big- box stores, people had to drive a few miles out of town for that. Wendy liked how they were close enough to the big city to have access to everything anyone could want, but far enough away to still have a small town feeling.

Wendy parked her car outside the shop and stepped out onto the sidewalk. She took a breath of the fresh, sea air. She was looking forward to this wedding. Anne and Rowan seemed to truly be in love, and Anne was a dream to work with. She was very agreeable but had enough of her own requests to make the wedding and ceremony feel very personal. Wendy stepped into the small bridal shop with a bright smile. She saw Anne excitedly waiting for her by the dressing rooms.

"Hi Wendy!" Anne said happily and ran over to give her a quick hug. Anne was practically glowing. Wendy had seen plenty of happy brides, but Anne seemed absolutely over the moon.

"I waited for you to get here before I tried it

on," Anne explained. "I'll just be a minute."

She followed one of the clerks from the shop into one of the large dressing rooms.

"So, you're the wedding planner, huh?" a voice said from just behind Wendy. Wendy spun around to face the mother of the groom, Celeste Coopers. Celeste had just returned from a vacation so Wendy only knew her from the newspaper and pictures she had seen of her. Wendy always made it her business to research everyone in the wedding party. This was for two reasons. It made the bride more comfortable if she felt her wedding planner was familiar with her family and loved ones. It also alerted Wendy to potential party animals, flakes, and other bad behaviors that might lead to a wedding disaster if not handled carefully. Celeste Coopers was a pillar of the community, very well-off, and very much involved in her sons' lives.

"Yes, I am," Wendy smiled warmly at her. "You must be Celeste, I'm Wendy," she offered her hand. Celeste reluctantly shook it.

"I don't get these new trendy jobs," Celeste commented shaking her head. "You base your entire career on people being too lazy to do things themselves. How is that working for you?"

Wendy was a little startled by the question. Despite the obvious rudeness of the woman's words, her tone was syrupy sweet as if she had just paid Wendy the nicest compliment.

"I enjoy my work very much," Wendy finally replied with a professional smile. She was not going to play into the woman's attempt to upset her. Celeste opened her mouth to speak again, but before she could the door to the dressing room swung open. Anne stepped out of the dressing room and took Wendy's breath away.

Anne was a beautiful woman to start with. She was petite with golden highlights in pin straight, light brown hair. She had bright blue eyes that always seemed eager to please. But she had a childish look about her, almost as if she was too young to even think about marriage. However, in the figure-hugging dress she had chosen she looked drop-dead gorgeous. She was absolutely transformed. The dress had a simple skirt, but the bodice was intricately woven with tiny glass beads that caught the reflection of the lights in the showroom.

"Wow!" Wendy breathed out with genuine awe.

"Do you like it?" Anne asked as she stepped into the middle of three mirrors. "I knew the moment that I put it on that this was the one," she sighed happily as she looked in the mirror.

"It's perfect," Wendy agreed.

Celeste clucked her tongue lightly and huffed as she rolled her eyes.

"Celeste, don't you like it?" Anne asked as she looked in the mirror at the reflection of her soon to be mother-in-law.

"What's to like?" Celeste asked and scrunched up her nose. "It looks just like any other dress that anyone would wear. I mean, they must have run it right off the same assembly line. You might as well be wearing a white sheet."

Wendy watched Anne's expression transform in the mirror. She went from the upturned lips, sparkling eyes, and rosy cheeks of elation, to a deep frown, downward cast eyes, and a blush of shame.

"I thought it was nice," she said softly.

"Sure, it's nice," Celeste muttered as if she was uttering a curse. "You there," she gestured to the clerk who had been helping Anne. "Bring me something a bit more fashionable, hmm?"

The woman stared at her for a moment, but nodded. Anne drew a deep breath and turned towards Celeste.

"I really like this dress, Celeste," she said.

Wendy observed quietly. She knew that a fight between family members could cause a wedding to be canceled. She also knew it wasn't her place to step in.

"I understand that, sweetheart, and I can't blame you for it, you just don't know any better," she smiled broadly as the clerk brought a high-end high-fashion dress that had angles so sharp Wendy wondered if it would be painful to wear. "Just try this one," she pressed.

Anne shifted from one foot to the other and then frowned. "Well, I guess it wouldn't hurt to try it," she said quietly.

Wendy bit her tongue and watched as Anne walked back into the dressing room with the new dress.

"Poor girl, she's a little behind on what's fashionable," Celeste muttered to the clerk. The clerk offered her a strained smile.

"Celeste, wedding dresses are very personal

to the bride," Wendy ventured casually. "Most brides fall in love with one dress, and that is the one they choose."

"That's because most brides don't have someone with the wisdom and fashion knowledge that I have," Celeste explained with a smirk. "Lucky for Anne, she has me."

Lucky wasn't the word Wendy would have used to describe the situation. But she kept that to herself. When Anne stepped out of the dressing room again, Wendy summoned a smile to her lips.

"You look beautiful, Anne," she said. But the truth was, the angles were falling against her subtle curves in all of the wrong places, making her look bulky rather than svelte.

"I tried it on," Anne said and cringed. "I still like the first one."

"Nonsense," Celeste said dismissively. "There is no comparing the quality. This is the dress for you."

"I don't know," Anne said hesitantly. "I really like how the other one looks on me."

"Well, anyone can look good in a tent, dear," Celeste said with a playful chuckle. "We'll just need to let this dress out a bit, you know, it's designed for the perfect body shape, but we can make it work for you with a little bit of effort. Can't we?" she asked the clerk with a tight smile.

Anne was staring with disbelief at Celeste. Wendy was waiting for the explosion. She was sure that Anne would lose it over the dress. Instead she cleared her throat and managed a smile.

"Well Celeste, you certainly know best about these types of things," Anne nodded. "We'll take this dress."

"Anne, are you sure?" Wendy asked with concern. "I know how much you loved the other one…"

"Stay out of this," Celeste snapped. "A daughter-in-law should trust the opinion of her mother-in-law more than they trust some fly-by-night wedding planner."

Wendy gritted her teeth. Anne had walked back to the dressing room to change. Wendy was so tempted to let Celeste have it. But it was Anne's wedding, and if she was willing to sacrifice what she wanted in order to keep the peace with Celeste, then Wendy had to respect her wishes and keep her mouth shut.

"It's nice that you two are so close," Wendy said politely and walked away from Celeste towards the clerk's desk.

"Yes, it is," Celeste said. She looked as if she was working up towards making another rude comment, so Wendy pretended to be receiving a call. She ducked out of the shop in order to get some air.

Wendy was not generally a violent person,

but Celeste certainly had a way of plucking her nerves. She took a deep breath and mentally coached herself to be calm and accepting of the situation. Celeste was right about one thing, she wasn't presenting herself as very professional if one busy-body mother-in-law was enough to make her lose her cool. She was just stepping back inside the shop when Anne and Celeste stepped out.

"Oh Wendy, just who I was looking for," Anne said with a smile. "I was wondering if you could tell us about the venue. Celeste wants to hear about it," she added with an apologetic frown.

Wendy smiled. "Of course she does, it's an important part of the wedding," she said quickly. She pulled out her tablet so that she could display pictures of the hotel as she spoke. "So, the venue we have chosen has a beautiful, spacious banquet room and hall that can be used for both the ceremony and the reception," Wendy explained. "But it also has the option for an outdoor wedding, which I know was something that you were considering."

"Yes, I thought it might be nice if the weather is good, which it usually is," Anne grinned.

"You can't seriously be considering that," Celeste said grimly as she batted her long lashes at Anne. "Are you aware that birds will most likely poop in your hair?" she asked.

Anne stared at her for a long moment. Wendy had to cover her mouth to suppress a laugh. Surely it would have been an amusing moment if it were not for the completely serious expression on Celeste's face.

"I hadn't thought of that," Anne said quietly.

"Well, that's what you have me for," Celeste said with a sniff in Wendy's direction. "Really, I don't know why a wedding planner would even suggest such a thing."

Wendy opened her mouth to defend herself but Anne just shook her head. Wendy almost jumped as a shrill ring came from Celeste's cell phone. It set her nerves on edge it was so loud.

"I'll get the car," Celeste said as she answered the call and walked towards her car. Wendy turned back to Anne.

"Anne, this is your wedding," she said gently. "I know that you are trying to be nice, but you really should get to wear the dress you love, and get married how you please."

"I know," Anne admitted with a sigh. "She's got her nose in everything. But the truth is that I don't really care what dress I wear, or where I get married, as long as I get to marry Rowan. He is the love of my life. I just want us to have a beautiful day, and that has nothing to do with all of these little things, does it?"

Wendy smiled at Anne's sentiment. "I couldn't agree with you more," she nodded. "But if you feel that you need me to stand up to Celeste a little more, just let me know."

"I just don't want to start a war," Anne explained. "I know that it just makes me look like a pushover, but I have a feeling no one has ever won a war against Celeste."

"You might be right about that," Wendy laughed softly. A horn blared, indicating that Celeste was waiting for Anne.

"I'll meet you tomorrow for the cake tasting," Anne said swiftly. "Rowan will be coming with me!"

"Fantastic," Wendy said and waved to her as she hurried towards the car. Wendy watched the pair pull off in Celeste's luxury sedan. She tried to have a positive attitude about the wedding, but instead she had a sinking feeling that things were not going to end well.

Chapter Two

Wendy spent the rest of her day reviewing the necessities for the wedding. She tried to avoid thinking about Celeste and her bad attitude. But her mind kept drifting back to it. The next morning she woke up looking forward to enjoying the cake tasting with Rowan and Anne. She did her best to put Celeste completely out of her mind. When she arrived at the little bakery that was providing the wedding cake, Wendy had a better attitude, until she stepped through the door and saw Celeste seated right between Anne and Rowan. Wendy clenched her teeth, plastered on a smile and walked confidently into the bakery.

"Hi all," she smiled at the three.

"Hi Wendy," Anne said with a broad smile. "Rowan, you remember Wendy, right?"

"Of course I do," Rowan smiled. "You're making our dream wedding come true."

Wendy laughed appreciatively and sat down across from Rowan, Anne, and Celeste. She did her best to hide her disappointment at Celeste's presence. Instead she focused on Rowan.

"Rowan, how are you?" she asked. "Did you find the tuxedo you wanted?"

"He's wearing a suit," Celeste said sharply. "A tuxedo is a costume, this isn't a costume party, it's a wedding."

Anne grimaced and stared at the table. Wendy cleared her throat and smiled. "Okay then," she nodded. "I've arranged a wide selection of cakes for you to try. Because well, the best part of picking a cake is taste testing, right?" she smiled warmly at the three. Rowan nodded and rubbed his hands together. Anne smiled enthusiastically. Celeste sat back in her chair and narrowed her eyes. Wendy gritted her teeth and gestured to the waitress to bring over the first selections.

"Oh, this is so dry," Celeste said and coughed dramatically. "Water? Is there water?" she called out plaintively as if she was about to die from thirst.

The bakery assistant hurried over with a glass of water.

"It doesn't seem dry to me," Rowan said with a frown.

"It's a little crumbly," Anne pointed out, obviously trying to support Celeste.

"Well, maybe we should focus on creamier cakes," Wendy suggested and nodded to the assistant. The next round of cakes was brought out. A small plate with a sample size of the cake was placed in front of each one of them. Before Anne could even take a bite of her cake, Celeste scrunched up her nose.

"Anne, maybe you should let Rowan take

over the taste testing," Celeste suggested.

"Huh?" Anne looked up at her with surprise, her fork poised above the cake she was about to taste. "Why?"

"Mom, what are you talking about?" Rowan asked with a touch of dread. Wendy glanced over at Celeste.

"I'm just asking if you really think it's such a good idea to stuff your face with so much cake right before the wedding?" Celeste frowned. "I mean, we wouldn't want to have to let the dress out again."

"We only had to let it out in the first place because you chose a new dress for me," Anne reminded her.

"Oh, I didn't choose it," Celeste laughed. "I would never choose your dress for you, Anne. I just showed you a better option. I am glad you came to your senses though."

"Mom, Anne can eat as much cake as she

wants," Rowan said and shook his head.

"Rowan, this doesn't concern you," Celeste said impatiently. "Men cannot possibly understand the pressure of putting on a few pounds. Only women can, right Anne? I mean how embarrassing would it be to be squeezed like a sausage into that beautiful dress?"

"Mom!" Rowan said sharply. Wendy watched as Rowan stood up from his chair. "This is getting out of hand, Mother. I'm not going to let you treat Anne the way you treat Suzette."

"Whatever do you mean?" Celeste asked and glared at her son. "This is how you speak to your mother? When we are out in public no less? You should be ashamed of yourself Rowan Matthew!"

Wendy glanced over at Anne whose cheeks were on fire. "It's okay, Rowan," she said softly. "Your mother is right. I shouldn't be eating all of this sugar. It might make me have a sugar crash, and there's so much to do. Why don't you do the tasting for me?" she suggested. "You know I trust your opinion."

Rowan looked angry but he sat back down in his chair. Wendy noticed that he shot a withering glare in Celeste's direction. "Fine," he said gruffly. "I liked the first one."

"The dry one?" Celeste gasped.

"Mother," Rowan shot her a dark look. "Anne said I should choose, and that's what I am choosing."

"Out of spite," Celeste snapped back. "Just because you know it is terrible, you're picking it."

"You know what," Rowan shoved his chair back from the table. "You pick the cake, Mother," he said and reached for Anne's hand. Anne hesitated. She looked from Wendy, to Celeste, then to Rowan. Wendy felt so much sympathy for the poor woman who looked a bit like a deer caught in headlights waiting for the inevitable.

"I think that's a wonderful idea," Wendy said warmly. "Celeste and I can choose a cake, and you and Anne can have a nice meal at the cafe next door. Does that sound good?"

"Lovely," Anne nodded with relief.

"I could eat," Rowan agreed, his voice still edged with frustration.

"Of course, leave me to do all of the work," Celeste sighed and rolled her eyes.

Wendy had to bite her tongue to keep from laughing. Celeste was so incredibly fussy that it was practically humorous. But Anne's worried expression, and Rowan's stormy gaze, reminded her that this was no joke. Celeste was practically torturing Anne, and seemed to be enjoying every moment of it.

"So Celeste, are you married?" Wendy asked as she took a bite of her cake.

"Not currently," Celeste replied and took a small bite of her cake.

"What was your wedding like?" Wendy asked. She hoped to broach the topic and perhaps convince Celeste that she should be more lenient with Anne's plans. But Celeste was not the least bit interested in conversation.

"This will do," she said with a shrug. "I'll be going now," she stood up from the table and walked right out of the bakery.

Wendy stared after her for a moment and then just shook her head. She ordered the cake that Celeste had chosen and then headed out of the bakery as well. She had plans to meet with a few of the vendors at the hotel where the wedding would be held. She was glad to get away from Celeste for a little while. She sent Anne a text to let her know that she was welcome to join her at the hotel if she'd like to discuss anything with the vendors. Then she drove to the hotel. When she arrived at the hotel she was swept up in the final confirmations for several things, from the catering, to the music, to the centerpieces. By the time she had a chance to take a breath, Anne had arrived.

"Did I miss everyone?" she asked. "Celeste insisted on joining us for lunch, and things took a little longer than expected."

"I have Lisa from Petals and More coming in to handle the flowers," Wendy explained with a smile. She had worked with her often and was looking forward to working with her again.

"Sounds perfect," Anne said with a smile. "I have to tell you that you have made all of this so pleasant for me, Wendy. You seem to have the magic touch to make everything turn out perfect."

"The important thing to remember, Anne, is that this wedding is about you and Rowan, no one else," Wendy reminded her and was about to bring up Celeste's interference when the woman herself walked through the door of the banquet hall.

"So, what's next on the agenda?" Celeste

asked immediately.

"The florist is coming in," Wendy said politely.

"And just who is this florist?" Celeste said with attitude.

"Lisa from Petals and More," Wendy explained trying to keep calm as she brought up some photos of her arrangements on her tablet.

"Oh, I don't know," Celeste said and scrunched up her nose as soon as she looked at the screen. "When Suzette and Chris got married my dear friend Beverly handled the flowers. The arrangements were unique, and classy. Not just a bunch of blooms thrown together."

"Trust me, Lisa does a wonderful job," Wendy said warmly.

"Well, of course you would say that," Celeste muttered. "You're obviously getting a kickback from promoting her as your florist."

"Celeste," Anne sighed and shook her head.

"Wendy knows what she is doing."

"Does she?" Celeste shrugged. "Have you seen this Lisa's work?" she asked.

"I have shown Anne these examples from previous weddings," Wendy interjected as she pointed at the screen. Her patience was beginning to wear thin. She was not as calm and accepting as Anne seemed to be. "She liked everything she saw. Didn't you Anne?"

"Yes, I did," Anne said with a brighter smile. "I am sure that she is the right florist for the wedding."

"But you can't be sure, can you?" Celeste asked as she narrowed her eyes. "I actually witnessed Beverly in action. I smelled her flowers, I know that they were fresh. There's nothing worse at a wedding than wilting flowers you know. That's just bad luck."

"Celeste," Anne said sharply, drawing a look of surprise from both Celeste and Wendy. "This is my wedding, and I want to use Wendy's florist."

Celeste's eyes widened. Her lips parted in a dramatic display of shock. She looked over at Wendy.

"Well, I do believe that Anne is getting a case of the Bridezilla," she laughed. "Of course it's your wedding, Anne. Who has ever implied that it wasn't?" she shook her head dismissively. Wendy was fuming. But when she looked over at Anne, she managed a smile.

"All right, let's let Wendy get back to work. Maybe I could use a glass of wine," Anne suggested.

Wendy was fascinated by how easily Anne shrugged Celeste off as if nothing she said or did had any impact on her. But Wendy knew better. It was wearing on Anne. She just hoped it wouldn't explode before the wedding, or worse, at the wedding. After Anne and Celeste headed for the hotel bar, Wendy breathed a sigh of relief and smiled as she looked over the room. At the moment it was nothing but white walls, high ceilings and some plain tables with white tablecloths. But she knew that when she and the rest of her crew were done with it, it would look very stylish and romantic.

"Hi, Wendy," a voice called out from the doorway of the banquet room. Wendy turned to see Lisa walking towards her with a large bouquet of flowers. "Sorry I am late I got held up thanking the manager for giving someone a job on my recommendation."

"That's okay," Wendy said with a smile. "We've been busy with other things."

"I brought you the sample you asked for," Lisa said as she showed Wendy the flowers. She had intertwined the lush, green stems and leaves with beaded lace and ribbons with subtle glitter that really made the flowers pop.

"They're beautiful," Wendy said as she studied them intently. "I really like the lace," she added. Lisa was always coming up with new and inventive ways to make the flowers a seamless part of the ceremony.

"So gorgeous," Anne squealed from the doorway. Wendy laughed as she nodded to Anne.

"I told you she's talented."

Rowan stepped in behind Anne. He had his fingers laced through hers as Wendy and Anne fussed over the flowers and complimented Lisa's work.

"Lisa, can I borrow this bouquet?" Wendy asked. "I just want to compare the shading to three choices of ribbons I have. I want to make sure the colors blend well."

"Of course," Lisa nodded. "In fact if you want me to look with you, I can let you know if we have any alternative flower colors that might work better."

"Perfect," Wendy nodded.

"Anne, I needed to ask if you had a song picked out for your first dance?" Wendy asked.

"Oh, no," Anne frowned. "I didn't even think about that."

"Do you and Rowan have a song that means something special to you?" Wendy asked hopefully.

"Not really," Anne shrugged. "We've never really gone out dancing."

"No worries," Wendy smiled. She flipped open her binder. "I just happen to have a CD here with a compilation of popular first dance songs, and a few of my favorites. Why don't you and Rowan take a drive around the neighborhood and see if you can pick one you both like?" she suggested.

"Okay," Anne nodded eagerly. She took the CD from Wendy and walked over to join Rowan.

Wendy smiled to herself when Rowan leaned close to kiss Anne softly. It was clear that he was in love with her. She was glad this would give the two of them some time alone together. She had a feeling that with Celeste around that was something they didn't get too often.

Rowan and Anne weren't gone for long before Celeste walked through the door. Wendy was right in the middle of discussing which material appeared to match best when she looked up to see just what she dreaded.

"Speak of the devil," she muttered under her breath as Celeste waltzed into the room. Wendy did her best to smile and muster a friendly tone.

"Hello, Celeste," she said. "I wasn't expecting you to come back."

"Clearly," Celeste said as she swept her gaze over the banquet room. "Are you planning on doing anything to improve this room?"

"Of course, it's not decorated, yet," Wendy

pointed out with a short laugh. "But I can promise you no birds will get in here."

"Don't be cute, Wendy," Celeste sniped and shook her head. "I just hope all of my friends will understand that I had nothing to do with any of this," she sighed. "It will be so embarrassing for them to see my son getting married this way."

With each word that Celeste spoke Wendy became more and more frustrated. She was about to give the woman a scathing lesson in manners, when Lisa piped up.

"Trust me, Wendy puts on the most amazing weddings," Lisa gushed. Wendy grimaced. She knew that Lisa was only trying to help. She also knew that Lisa had just painted a target on her own forehead.

"And who are you?" Celeste asked as she turned to look at her.

"My name is Lisa," Lisa smiled. "I'm the florist."

"Not anymore you're not," Celeste said casually. "I have someone else coming in to take care of it."

Lisa stared at Celeste, obviously shocked.

"Celeste, Anne agreed that she wanted Lisa to do the flowers," Wendy said sternly. "We've already coordinated them with the material for the ribbons and tablecloths."

"That hideous bouquet?" Celeste shook her head. "My boys, they both went for looks over brains. Unfortunately, sometimes I have to clean up their messes."

Wendy was furious, but as she moved to speak, Lisa spoke before she could.

"I'm sorry if you don't like the bouquet," Lisa said quietly. "I have many other options to choose from."

"Listen to me you little corner store peddler," Celeste said and stepped closer to Lisa. "The only option I want from you, is the option to pretend I never laid eyes on you. Now get out of my sight before I buy your little shop and put you out of business, to be honest it would be an act of charity," she snapped her hand sharply to the side, indicating that Lisa should leave the room.

"Celeste, that is completely uncalled for," Wendy protested and stepped between Celeste and Lisa. "Unless Anne tells me that she would prefer a different florist, I can't allow you to terminate the contract I have already agreed to with Lisa."

"Blah, blah, blah," Celeste rolled her eyes. "Anne will do exactly what I tell her to do. Beverly will be here any minute with the samples I requested. Really, who thinks lilacs are good at a wedding?" she shook her head.

Lisa turned away from Wendy and Celeste. She tried to disguise the fact that she was visibly upset by how she had been spoken to. Lisa was usually nothing less than professional, but Celeste had a way of cutting straight to the core with her words.

"These are the flowers that Anne chose," Wendy said flatly.

"Yes, they are," Anne said as she stepped into the room. Her arm was curled around Rowan's. "Celeste, what do you think you're doing?" she asked with obvious frustration.

"I am just making some better arrangements," Celeste explained. "This florist has no real experience with the type of high end wedding that we are planning. I'm just trying to save you some embarrassment, Anne."

"Celeste, this is ridiculous," Anne said. She was clearly exasperated. Wendy braced herself as she was sure all of Anne's pent up frustration would explode.

"Excuse me?" Celeste snapped. "Are you speaking to me in that tone?"

Anne stared at her with hatred in her eyes. It was surprising to see, considering that Anne had been so accepting and calm previously. Wendy assumed she had finally had enough.

"Rowan, aren't you going to do anything about your mother?" Anne asked as she looked at him. Rowan stared between the two women with a grimace of fear.

"Well, I don't know, Anne," he stammered. "Beverly did do a good job on the flowers for Suzette and Chris' wedding."

"Are you serious?" Anne spat out.

"Calm down, Anne, you're making a scene," Celeste offered a fake laugh and cleared her throat.

"That's it!" Anne suddenly shouted. "I don't care about the flowers, or the dress, or the cake! I don't care about any of this. I'm not sure if I can marry a man who can't stand up to his own mother!" she spat out her final words in Rowan's direction.

"Anne, wait!" Rowan said desperately and

started to go after her. Anne charged off through the door of the banquet hall. Celeste grabbed her son by the arm and pulled him back.

"Let her go, boy," she mumbled. "She's just having one of those pre-wedding meltdowns, she'll be fine once she has her little tantrum."

"Tantrum?" Rowan snapped and shook her grasp off his arm. "You know what, Mother, you are a horrible person. I am not going to lose my wife because you can't mind your own business!"

With that he stalked off after Anne. Wendy cringed. Celeste grasped at her scarf and fiddled with it nervously.

"Well, I guess tantrums aren't reserved only for brides, grooms can have them, too," she muttered and shook her head. "I'm sorry you two had to witness such an ugly scene. But you heard Anne, she doesn't care about the flowers. So, Beverly will be handling them. Really, Lisa, you're the one that caused this entire fight. If you had just taken my direction and admitted that you were in over your head, then no one would have needed to get upset."

She shook her head and walked out of the banquet hall. Lisa was left staring after her, slack-jawed with tears of confusion in her eyes.

"Lisa, I'm so sorry," Wendy said with a frown. "Please don't worry, I'll talk to Anne about the job and make sure she stays with you."

"Don't bother," Lisa shook her head and snatched up the flowers she had left on the table. "You couldn't pay me enough to be in the same room with that woman again."

She stalked off. Wendy was left alone in the banquet hall. She felt as if she had just been hit by a truck. Not only was she going to have to deal with an entirely new florist, the wedding itself seemed to be in jeopardy. Wendy knew that she was going to have to work some of her magic if the wedding was going to go ahead as planned.

***

By the time Wendy left the hotel her nerves were on edge. She felt as if she was losing control of the wedding, and that disaster was inevitable. She needed a chance to clear her mind. She drove back to her condo and parked. As she was stepping out of her car her phone began to ring. When she saw that it was Brian calling she answered it right away.

"Hi beautiful, how is your day going?" Brian asked in his charming but slightly gruff tone.

"You will not believe the day I've had," Wendy nearly exploded into the phone. "I'm sorry," she said quickly as she realized how harsh she sounded. "I just have never had this much difficulty with a wedding before."

"Is your client giving you a hard time?" he

asked with sympathy.

"It's not even her," Wendy sighed. "It's the groom's mother. She's driving me up the wall. She's the most spoiled, self-centered, judgmental, cruel person I have ever met," she huffed as she took off her shoes. She hung them lightly from one hand and held her phone with the other. She needed to feel the sand beneath her feet to calm herself down a little.

"I'm so sorry you're having such a hard time," Brian said. "I was going to see if you'd like to go to dinner, but I'm guessing that's not the best idea?"

"Honestly, I have to figure out a way to get this entire family on the same page or this wedding is going to fall apart," Wendy sighed. "I would love to go to dinner with you, but I won't be able to relax and enjoy our time together if I'm worried about the wedding."

"I understand," Brian replied. "Try not to let it

get to you too much, Wendy. You do an amazing job, but you can't expect every wedding to be perfect."

"You're right," Wendy said softly. But as she caught sight of the waves crashing against the sand, and as the laughter of people enjoying the beach carried through the breeze, she knew she was lying. She did expect every wedding to be perfect. In her mind it should be the one perfect day in everyone's life. She was certain that with a little bit of togetherness she could make it happen. After she said goodbye to Brian she took a few minutes to observe the rush and retreat of the waves. Then she headed inside to set her plan into action.

Chapter Three

Anne had decided to have a rehearsal lunch, even though a dinner was more traditional, as she wanted to be fresh on her wedding day. The rehearsal lunch was two days away and Wendy knew that everyone's schedules would be tight, but she hoped her emergency invites would gather all of the family members together. First she called the caterer to see if she could add a dinner the next night. Then she called Anne.

"Hello?" Anne said tearfully.

"Anne, are you okay?" Wendy asked swiftly.

"I don't know," Anne replied honestly. "I can't believe this is happening."

"Just take a deep breath, Anne, don't make any big decisions while you're upset," Wendy advised. "I've just heard from the caterer who would like to host a dinner for just the family members before the rehearsal lunch. Do you think you would be up for that tomorrow night?"

"A dinner before the lunch?" Anne hesitated. "I don't know, Wendy, everyone is pretty upset."

"Trust me, Anne," Wendy said gently. "Sometimes the best way to deal with our problems is just to air them out."

"I know that Rowan and I can be there," Anne said. "We talked about what happened today, and things are thin but better than they were. I can't promise the same for Celeste though, neither of us have heard a word from her."

"What about your father?" Wendy suggested. "Would he be able to be there?"

"I think so," Anne answered. "I will check with him."

"Thanks, Anne," Wendy said appreciatively. "Try not to worry too much, okay?"

"I'll try," Anne replied shakily. After Wendy hung up the phone with Anne she dialed

Celeste's number. Wendy fully expected to have to leave a message, but Celeste answered on the second ring.

"Well, if it isn't Wendy the Wedding Wrecker," Celeste said in a nasty tone. "What can I do for you?"

Wendy narrowed her eyes but kept her voice friendly. "Celeste, I'm calling to invite you to a special dinner that the caterer would like to host for just the family tomorrow night. Do you think you could make it?"

"What's the point?" Celeste asked. "We both know that this wedding isn't going to happen."

"That's where you're wrong, Celeste," Wendy said as calmly as she could. "I know that this wedding is going to happen, whether you are part of it or not. Can you really say that you would rather miss out on your son's wedding than come to a simple dinner?"

"What time?" Celeste asked. "I can't promise

anything, but I'll think about it."

Wendy gave her the details of the dinner and then hung up. Part of her wished that Celeste would not bother to show up, but she knew better. Celeste needed to be in control, no matter what. Wendy finished making the calls to the groom's brother and his wife. Once she had everything arranged she settled down at her desk and began making a plan of action. She knew that whatever happened, everything would have to go off without a hitch at this dinner, or Celeste might be proven right, there might not be any wedding to plan.

***

When Wendy arrived at the banquet hall the following evening, she found that the caterer had put together exactly what she had requested. With a little bit of research Wendy had been able to find out some of the family member's favorite drinks and foods so that the meal could set a jovial mood. However, this did nothing to melt the icy glares that Celeste and most of her family, as well as Anne, were exchanging as they arrived.

The one bright spot was Arnold Max, who was Anne's elderly father. Anne had been a late in life baby for her mother who had passed when she was in her teens. He was sweet, and flirting with the waitress as well as teasing his daughter about her future as a wife and mother. He seemed oblivious to the anger that was circulating through everyone in attendance.

"Thank you all for coming," Wendy said as she welcomed them. "I know this was last minute, so it means a lot that you were able to come. Now, I know there are some kinks to work out in the wedding plans, but tonight is not about the wedding. Tonight is about two families joining together. It's a chance to get to know each other a little better, share some delicious food and wine, and relax."

Celeste rolled her eyes as Wendy expected, but everyone else seemed to be warmed by her speech. Still, the tension was thick in the room as everyone sat down at the table. There was not even a whisper of greeting amidst the group. Wendy felt her stomach twist. It wasn't often that she had to fight against such a cold family, but she knew that she could fix things with the right effort. She gestured to the waitress who brought over what Wendy knew to be Celeste's favorite wine. It had cost her quite a penny, but she hoped that it would help the woman to relax a little and be a little kinder.

"What's this? Wine?" Celeste asked instantly as the wine was poured. "Well, how very insensitive of you, Wendy," she growled.

Wendy had just sat down at the table. She lifted her eyes to meet Celeste's, absolutely stunned by her words and her demeanor.

"I thought you would like it," she managed to get out.

"Sure, it's my favorite," Celeste said knowingly. "But Suzette is an alcoholic, out of respect for her, we shouldn't have wine at the table."

"What?" Suzette cried out with fury. "Celeste, I am not an alcoholic!"

"Oh, sweetheart, being in denial doesn't make it any less true," Celeste said and rolled her eyes. "We are all just trying to help you."

"Chris?" Suzette said as she looked over at her husband. "Do you hear what your mother is saying to me?"

"I do," he mumbled and glanced over at Celeste. "Mom, give it a rest, will you?"

"Enabling," Celeste sung out and took a big swallow of her wine. Suzette followed suit by downing half of her glass. Wendy was still reeling from the interaction.

Anne made a small noise of disapproval in her throat and turned in her chair so that she was only engaged with her father. Rowan and Chris were both scowling at their mother, and Suzette seemed to be in a race to polish off the first bottle of wine.

As the sniping and arguing continued to escalate, Wendy decided she needed to alert the security staff that there might be some problems.

"Excuse me for a few moments," Wendy said as she pushed her chair back from the table. No one seemed to notice as they squabbled amongst each other. Wendy grimaced and hurried out of the banquet hall.

The security office was near the lobby, set back from the main hallway. Wendy knocked lightly on the door and then opened it. She was greeted by a bank of monitors, as well as a burly man sitting behind a semi-circle desk. "Sorry to bother you," Wendy said as the man turned to look at her.

"No problem," he replied with a kind smile. He nodded his head towards the camera that was recording the banquet room. "Looks like things are getting a little iffy in there."

"Yes, that's why I'm here," Wendy explained. "I just wanted to let you know we might be needing some security guards in the banquet room if things keep getting worse."

"Family," the man shrugged with a short laugh. "It always brings out the best and the worst in us."

"I guess so," Wendy frowned and shook her head. "I'm going to try to cool everyone off, but I just thought I'd give you a heads up. I didn't realize that there was a camera in the banquet room."

"Oh yes, we recently upgraded the system," the man explained. "We've got cameras in every hallway, and every public area. Obviously not in the guest rooms," he explained. "But no one can really get anywhere in this place without being recorded."

"Good to know," Wendy frowned. She didn't actually like the idea of being constantly recorded, but she could understand the hotel's need for the precaution.

"If you need anything, just let me know," the man said and offered his hand. "My name is Marcus, I'm the security expert around here."

"Thank you, Marcus," Wendy said as she shook his hand in return. "It's good to know that I'm not the only one keeping an eye on the situation."

"I'm watching over you," he assured her with a warm smile.

Wendy made her way slowly back towards the banquet hall. She was fairly certain she would have to pull people apart when she stepped through the door. She opened the door and stepped inside to the sound of a roar. But the roar had nothing to do with anger, and everything to do with laughter. Stunned, Wendy looked over the people at the table. Everyone was laughing, even Celeste.

"And that's how I finally got that pig to stay in the pen, whether she liked it or not," Arnold chuckled and winked at Wendy. Wendy winked back, even though she didn't know what the story was about. Whatever it was had broken the tension at the table, and for that she was very grateful. As she sat back down at the table, Arnold eased himself up out of his chair. He leaned on the table for a moment, and then straightened up so that he could speak clearly.

"I have something for my little girl, and her future husband," he explained. "I would like to present to you something that has been passed down through our family for generations," her father said with a fragile smile. "I know your mother would have wanted to be the one to give it to you, as she was the one who received it from my mother, but unfortunately she can't do that," he frowned. Anne dabbed at her eyes with her napkin. "So, your old man will just have to stumble his way through it," he muttered. "After the vows are said, after the ceremony is over, we have the celebration. Cutting into the cake for the first time, is like opening up that celebration of the rest of your life. This cake-cutting knife," he held the box out to Anne, "has been part of our celebrations for so many years. It is filled with the love and hopes of many couples, and now it belongs to you and your soon-to-be husband," he smiled warmly at Rowan.

Anne opened the box and pulled out an antique silver cake-cutting knife. It glinted in the lights over the table. It had intricate swirls engraved on it.

"Oh, Dad, it's beautiful," Anne said happily as she looked up at him. "Thank you so much."

"Yes, thank you," Rowan said with a kind smile. "It will be something very special that we can pass down in our own family. I look forward to it being part of our tradition," he added.

"I'm glad, Rowan," Arnold smiled in return. "I know that Anne's mother would have been very proud of the woman she's become, and the man she is about to marry."

With the warmth at the table growing, Wendy began to relax. She felt as if a crisis had been avoided, but not because of her actions. Arnold was the one that should have all of the credit. Just as she was raising her glass of wine in a toast to Arnold's words however, Celeste began to speak.

"Yes, that is a lovely gesture, Arnold," she said with a slight frown. "But I'm afraid I've already ordered a set to be used at the wedding."

Wendy locked eyes with Celeste. She had talked to Anne about ordering a set but Anne knew about the knife, and had hoped that her father would be passing it down to her, and so she had refused to order anything.

"That's very kind of you, Celeste, but this one has sentimental value, I'm sure you understand," Anne said cautiously.

Wendy could tell that Anne, like her, was worried about everything blowing up into an argument once more. In fact everyone at the table seemed to be bracing themselves for Celeste's reaction to Anne's words. Celeste picked up her napkin and lightly dabbed at her lips, which did not have a crumb on them.

"Of course I understand, my dear," Celeste said softly, then set her napkin down. "All families have traditions," she added and reached out to lightly pat the back of Anne's hand. "I would never dream of interfering with that."

"Thank you," Anne said with relief. As their glasses of wine were refilled, the laid-back energy of a few moments before returned to the table. Even Celeste seemed to be having a great time. As the dinner wound down and the waitress began collecting the dishes, Wendy was beginning to get excited for the wedding again. If they could just get through one more day without any huge disaster then everything would be fine. As everyone was leaving the hotel, Wendy was careful not to let Celeste and Anne be alone together. She had a feeling that Celeste wasn't as understanding as she was pretending to be. She didn't want any blow-up to occur.

"Goodnight, Anne," Celeste said and kissed her cheek. "I look forward to the rehearsal lunch tomorrow. I'm sure that you'll love the arrangements that Beverly made."

"Beverly?" Anne asked with surprise. "But Lisa was the one providing the flowers," Anne frowned.

"Well dear, you said you didn't care," Celeste reminded her. "Remember, when you were throwing your little fit?"

"Good night, Celeste," Wendy interrupted quickly before things could escalate. "I think Anne needs her rest, don't you?"

"Hmph," Celeste shrugged and walked away. Once she was out of earshot Anne turned to Wendy.

"I'm so sorry, I didn't know that she had actually brought Beverly in, I could just..."

"Anne, it's okay," Wendy smiled warmly. "I've looked at the flowers Beverly is providing, and they are just as beautiful. It will be perfect."

"But Lisa is your friend," Anne reminded her.

Wendy frowned. She didn't have the heart to tell Anne that Lisa had refused to work with Celeste or be anywhere near her. She also knew that letting Celeste have that win might be enough to satisfy the woman and keep her from demanding control in other areas of the wedding.

"Lisa had some prior engagements," Wendy explained. "She understood that Celeste preferred the other florist."

"You mean she didn't want to do the wedding after the scene we put on?" Anne said, reminding Wendy of her keen perception.

"All that matters now is everyone is getting along, and you are a couple of days away from the wedding," Wendy smiled. "No need to stress over a florist, what's done is done, and the flowers will be wonderful. I hope that you are able to enjoy your wedding day for the magical day that it is."

"I think I will be able to," Anne replied with a small smile. "My father reminded me of just how important it is to be kind, and generous. I think Celeste must have had a very difficult life for her to be so miserable."

"That's probably true," Wendy nodded, impressed by Anne's ability to have compassion for Celeste even after everything she had said and done to hurt her. "Get some rest, Anne,"

Wendy smiled warmly. "Your big day will be here soon."

"Thanks, Wendy," Anne replied and gave her a quick hug before walking off.

***

On her drive home, Wendy's phone chimed. She glanced at it to see that it was a text from Celeste. She left it until she arrived home at her condo and had parked her car. Then she looked at it again.

Please confirm the cocktails between the wedding and dinner.

Wendy raised an eyebrow. It was late, but she knew how fussy Celeste was, so she sent back a menu of what drinks would be available to the guests. She was just getting out of her car when her phone chimed again. She expected it to be a thank you note from Celeste for sending the menu. It was a text from Celeste but it definitely did not say thank you.

Not acceptable, we need more high end drinks. Please give this list to your bartender, if he can't make the drinks, then we need to find someone else.

Wendy was very confused. Just a little while ago Celeste had been angry that there was wine at the table, now she was demanding certain cocktails. She could only put it down to Celeste being as difficult as possible. Wendy couldn't even imagine trying to find a skilled bartender on a day's notice. Wendy decided to ignore the text for the night and headed into the condo. After the fourth question mark text, Wendy turned her phone off and set it down beside her bed. She took being rested for the weddings she planned very seriously. Now that the confirmations were done and the final selections had been made, she could feel confident about getting a few hours of solid sleep. She nestled into her pillows and closed her eyes.

Chapter Four

When Wendy woke up the next morning her heart was instantly pounding. She rarely felt anxious about the weddings she planned any more, other than that expected twinge that she hoped everything went well. However, when she sat up in bed, she had a terrible feeling. She picked up her phone and turned it on. Immediately, notifications of about fifteen texts came through.

Each and every one of them was from Celeste. Wendy shook her head as she reviewed them. All were petty demands about the wedding, from ensuring the wine glasses were a certain height, to requesting a specific brand of runner for the bride to walk down. Wendy tucked her phone away, determined not to answer her right away. She tried to reassure herself that this was good news, as it meant that Celeste had accepted that the wedding would go ahead.

After a quick shower Wendy dressed and sat down in her office. She began going through Celeste's texts slowly and responding to them with what she could and couldn't do the day before the wedding. Wendy was hoping the rehearsal lunch would go as smoothly as the family dinner had the night before. She contacted everyone in the wedding party who would be attending the lunch to ensure they would be there. Then she selected a dress to wear for the lunch. She hated to admit it but Celeste's critical eye played a part in her choice.

The rest of the morning was filled with last minute wedding activities. Wendy was caught up in a dilemma with one of the musicians for the ceremony and didn't realize the time. It was just after one and the rehearsal lunch started at one.

Wendy's heart began racing as she realized that she had left the group unsupervised. As she was getting dressed and putting on her makeup she texted Anne to let her know she would be arriving soon, but received no response. Then she texted Celeste in an attempt to keep the peace. She walked to her car as fast as she could as she tried not to trip over in her high heels.

"Wendy," she turned to see Mrs. Sykes, her lovely but overly talkative neighbor, calling out to her.

"Mrs. Sykes," Wendy said quickly. "I'm sorry but I can't talk now," she said in a rush as she continued walking to her car. "I'm late for lunch."

"Oh, okay, nothing urgent, I'll speak to you tomorrow," she said with a smile as she waved to her.

"Thanks, Mrs. Sykes," Wendy called out as she reached her car. She checked her phone. Neither Anne nor Celeste had texted her back. Wendy frowned and tried calling Anne's cell phone number. It went straight to voicemail. She left a message, and then tried Celeste's number. It rang a few times and then it went to voicemail.

Wendy felt a sudden sense of urgency. She started her car and rushed to get to the hotel. All kinds of possibilities played through her mind as she battled traffic to get to the rehearsal lunch. Had Anne decided against the wedding after all? Had Celeste caused some kind of drama that had caused everyone to flee? Or, was Wendy just reading too much into it, and perhaps the two women had ignored their cell phones in honor of the lunch, that she was late for. When she arrived at the hotel she was relieved to see that it was still there. She parked and hurried into the lobby. Then she continued straight to the banquet hall. In her mind she visualized a happy scene, with everyone laughing and celebrating while sharing delicious food. She pushed open the door with this scene in mind.

That was not the scene that greeted her. The table was abandoned, with the members of the wedding party scattered around the room whispering softly to one another. Wendy could see their looks of concern and embarrassment, and she soon discovered the reason for those expressions. She could hear Anne quietly crying.

"What is going on?" Wendy asked with grave concern as she walked further into the banquet hall. Anne was standing just beside Suzette. Her face was streaked with what remained of her make-up, her eyes were red rimmed and swollen. Wendy glanced around the room but she saw no sign of Rowan or Chris. "What's wrong, Anne? What's happened?"

"I can't believe her, I just can't believe her," Anne said between sobs. "She is a horrible, terrible woman, and I can't do this anymore."

Wendy frowned and gave Anne a gentle hug. "Take a breath, sweetie, it's the day before your wedding, there's a lot of stress. Just try to slow down, and tell me what happened. I'm sure we can fix it."

"I doubt it with that bitch," Suzette rolled her eyes.

"My cake-cutting knife," Anne gulped out. "I had it here so we could display it today at the rehearsal lunch. She stalked in here, she took my knife, and left this one," she held up a silver cake-cutting knife. It was engraved with the date of the wedding and the initials of the bride and groom. It was a decent knife, but it certainly wasn't the ornate antique knife that had been handed down through Anne's family. "I didn't fight her on the dress. I didn't fight her on the tuxedo, or the menu, or anything that she took control over. This is the one thing I wanted," she wiped at her eyes and shook her head. Wendy quickly handed her a tissue from her purse.

"I know you must think I'm being silly," Anne sniffled. "But I just can't take much more. I'm not even sure that I want to go through with the wedding."

"Oh no, don't say that," Wendy said quickly.

She took the knife from Anne and tucked it into her purse. "Let me go find Celeste. I'll give this back to her, and get you your knife. She is not going to ruin this day for you, Anne, not if there's anything I can do to stop it."

"Thank you, Wendy," Anne said and wiped at her eyes. "I so badly want to marry Rowan, but if it's going to be like this for the rest of our lives, I just don't know."

"Where is Rowan?" Wendy asked as she glanced around.

"He went off with his brother somewhere," Suzette waved her hand dismissively. She lost her balance slightly when she did. Wendy narrowed her eyes as she looked at the woman closely.

"Suzette, have you been drinking?" Wendy asked cautiously.

"It's a party, isn't it?" Suzette shot back with annoyance. "Let me get you a nice, tall glass of wine, Anne darling," Suzette said with a smirk. "You're going to need it in this family, trust me."

Wendy frowned, but she knew that a drink wouldn't be the worst thing for Anne at the moment. Wendy might even consider joining them after she spoke to Celeste. She stepped out into the hallway outside the banquet hall. The hotel was large, but most of the guest facilities were on the first floor. Unless Celeste had left the hotel, Wendy was hoping that some old fashioned paging would help her find the woman. She began repeatedly dialing Celeste's cell phone number.

Instead of waiting for her to answer, as Wendy expected she wouldn't, she listened closely for the woman's shrill ring tone that had annoyed her to no end since the first time she heard it. She didn't hear anything at first, until she turned down a short hallway. There were only four rooms off the hallway, and a small reading area with a clock and shelf above a wooden table. It was just a little nook where people from the banquet hall could retreat to if things got too noisy. Wendy could hear the ring tone. It was coming from one of the rooms on the left side of the hall. In fact it was coming from the room which had a little sign hanging from it declaring that it was closed for maintenance. Wendy reached for the doorknob.

"Celeste?" she called out, and then waited a moment. She didn't want to walk in on the woman in an embarrassing situation. When she heard no response she dialed her number once more. She heard the shrill ring tone on the other side of the door.

Carefully, Wendy turned the knob on the door. The first thing she noticed was the smell of strong fumes. The walls had recently been painted and were still in the process of drying. There were still plastic drop cloths on the floor, and paint cans scattered about. In the middle of all of this, was a splash of crimson. Wendy thought it was paint at first. Then it dawned on her that the walls were being painted white. There would be no reason for red paint. She followed the splash with her eyes until it led to Celeste, laying face up on the floor, with the antique cake-cutting knife sticking out of her chest.

Chapter Five

Wendy crouched down beside Celeste's body, and felt her stomach churn. She could tell that she was dead, but she still had to check to see if there was a pulse. She found Celeste's skin still warm to the touch, but there was no evidence of a pulse.

With a trembling hand Wendy pulled her cell phone out of her purse and dialed the police. She reported the name of the hotel and the location of the body, as well as the name of the person who had been killed. As soon as she hung up with the police, she stood up and dialed Brian's phone number. She waited impatiently for him to answer, her heart pounding against her chest.

"Did you miss me?" Brian asked in a smug tone.

"Brian," Wendy breathed out desperately

before he could even finish. "Something terrible has happened!"

"What?" Brian asked with immediate urgency in his voice. "Are you okay? Are you in trouble?"

"I'm okay," Wendy replied breathlessly. "But the mother of the groom is dead, she's been murdered."

"Celeste? The woman that you've been telling me about?" Brian asked swiftly. "Are you safe?"

"I think so," Wendy replied. "I just found her body, I've called the police."

"Wendy, stay right there until the police arrive," Brian instructed. "Only tell them how you found the body, nothing more, understand me?"

"I do," Wendy replied fearfully. She had been falsely accused of a crime before, and she had learned her lesson about saying too much to the police. Wendy was paralyzed by her discovery.

She thought she should tell Anne, she should tell Rowan, and Chris, but she couldn't bring herself to dial her phone. She couldn't bring herself to leave the room. Somewhere in the middle of all of the emotional chaos in her mind she realized that now there would certainly be no wedding. Celeste, despite her murder not being her fault, had still managed to get what she wanted.

The police arrived quickly and after a few quick but thorough questions, which Wendy answered very carefully, they escorted Wendy out of the room with an order not to go far. Wendy stood in the hallway, still in a state of shock. As more police officers and the medical examiner arrived, Anne and Rowan came walking down the hallway hand in hand. They were looking curiously at the gathering of police and officials.

"Wendy, why are all the police here?" Anne asked with some concern. Wendy looked from Anne to Rowan, who did not yet know that his mother was dead. It made her feel sick to her stomach all over again to be the one that had to break the news.

"I'm sorry to be the one to tell you this, but I just found Celeste," she hesitated a moment and lowered her eyes. "She's been killed."

"What?" Rowan shouted drawing the attention of a few of the police officers.

"Celeste?" Anne repeated, her eyes wide. Her face drained of color as she looked over at Rowan. "How?"

"That's not possible," Rowan stammered out. "Nothing could kill that woman," his eyes were glazed with emotion, but what kind of emotion Wendy couldn't quite determine.

"We have a few questions," one of the officers said sharply as soon as he was informed of who Anne and Rowan were.

Wendy was nudged out of the way as the officers began interviewing Rowan and Anne.

She knew that she shouldn't get in the middle of the investigation, but she was so intrigued that she listened in as much as she could.

"Where were you in the last hour?" one of the officers asked as he pulled Anne away from Rowan.

"After Celeste took my knife, I went for a walk," Anne whispered. "I was upset."

"Why were you upset?" the officer asked.

"I had an argument with Celeste," Anne admitted and fought back tears. "I needed to cool off."

"Did anyone go on this walk with you?" the officer narrowed his eyes.

"No," Anne shook her head slowly. "I was alone. Then I returned to the banquet hall, and that was when Wendy arrived. She told me she would take care of it, that she would get the knife back and talk to Celeste."

Wendy felt her heart sink. She could tell from

the line of questioning that Anne would be a suspect. Of all the people that had flashed through Wendy's mind as potential suspects, Anne had not been one of them. Even knowing that she had no alibi for the murder, Wendy still didn't believe she was capable of the crime but then again people often surprised her. Her phone chimed, alerting her to a text. She checked it to discover that Brian had arrived at the hotel. She walked out to the lobby to meet him.

"They've got just about every officer on the police force out here," Brian said grimly. "This is a huge case."

"Celeste was very well known," Wendy nodded slightly. "I haven't seen Officer Polson," Wendy said. Wendy had come to know Officer Polson in less than ideal circumstances, when she had been arrested by him for murder. She thought she might be able to get some information from him.

"He's on leave." Brian nodded. "You found her?" Brian asked softly though he already knew the answer to that question. "Are you handling it okay?"

"I think so," Wendy replied nervously.

Brian's hazel eyes were clouded with emotion as they intently peered into hers. "Please tell me you have an alibi."

Wendy's eyes widened. She hadn't even thought of herself as being a suspect in the crime. But the more she considered it, the more she realized she would be. After the words she'd had with Celeste, she was just as likely to want to harm the woman as anyone else. She thought for a few moments trying to piece together the time frame and she realized that luckily she did have an alibi.

"Well, from what I've heard they think the murder occurred in the last hour or so. Celeste stormed out with the cake knife when the guests saw her alive. So, yes I do have an alibi. I was at home, my neighbor, Mrs. Sykes, saw me leaving and then I came straight here, spoke to Anne and then found Celeste," Wendy said quickly. "But Anne doesn't have an alibi."

"Anne, the bride?" Brian asked and cocked an eyebrow. "Do you think she was involved?"

"Absolutely not," Wendy replied and shook her head. "She's a sweet woman, wouldn't harm a fly."

"But you said that Celeste was practically torturing her throughout this process," Brian reminded her. "Maybe she just couldn't take it anymore."

"No," Wendy said firmly. "I just can't believe that."

"You won't," Brian corrected in a murmur.

"What?" Wendy asked with annoyance.

"Look Wendy, I'm just saying, you've grown to like this woman. Sometimes it's hard to think of someone we care for as being capable of such a terrible crime," he explained and took her hand gently in his.

"That's not what's happening here," Wendy said firmly. "I just know she couldn't do this." But Wendy also knew that as nice as Anne seemed, a woman like Celeste could push anyone over the edge. She just wasn't going to admit that to Brian.

"Okay," Brian nodded. "Well, I can guarantee you that the police are going to want to interview everyone that was involved. I'm sure they won't make an arrest until that is completed."

As he finished speaking two officers began walking through the lobby. Held between them, shaking and sobbing, was Anne.

Wendy stared with shock as the officers walked past and out the door of the lobby.

"I stand corrected," Brian said with surprise.

"How can they be doing this?" Wendy

demanded. "How can they just arrest her like that?"

"Maybe she confessed," Brian suggested, obviously baffled himself.

"No, Anne wouldn't have confessed to something she didn't commit," Wendy insisted.

"Maybe they are just taking her in for further questioning. Let me see what I can find out," Brian said and gave her hand a light squeeze. Wendy watched him walk away. Rowan had walked into the lobby accompanied by another police officer. Wendy moved closer to overhear what they were saying.

"I don't care what the evidence says my fiancée didn't do this," Rowan insisted.

"Sir, I know it can be shocking to think of something like this, but I need you to think very hard about whether or not there were some signs that Anne was plotting to kill your mother," the officer explained in a calm tone.

"This is nuts, just nuts," Rowan growled. "I want to know where they are taking her, when can I see her? I'm calling my lawyer right now," he said gruffly and whipped out his cell phone. Wendy was relieved to hear that Rowan was not convinced of his fiancée's guilt.

She could only hope that he wouldn't be the only one to feel that way. When Brian came back a few minutes later, he had a grave expression.

"There's a problem," he said in a murmur and pulled her aside from the crowd of police officers and onlookers.

"What is it?" Wendy asked nervously.

"Well, she hasn't been arrested, but she is being taken down to the station for further questioning because she is their prime suspect," Brian said. "Unless something new comes to light in her defense I think it is only a matter of time before they arrest her."

"But why?" Wendy asked.

"Well, the argument they had, she has no alibi and apparently someone saw her enter the room where Celeste was murdered around the time the murder occurred," Brian stated.

"Who," Wendy gasped.

"They wouldn't say," he said as he shook his head. "Anne claims that she never entered the room but she has no alibi."

"But there must be a mistake," Wendy exclaimed. "I don't believe she would ever do this."

"I hope you're right," Brian said not looking convinced.

"Will you help me, Brian?" Wendy asked as she studied him. "I know you're busy, you have your own cases, and no one has hired you to look into this one."

Brian ran his hands lightly from her elbows down to her hands and held them in his own. "Wendy, I would do anything to help you. But even if we do figure out who the murderer is, that won't save the wedding."

"I know it won't," Wendy shook her head. "It's not about the wedding, it's never really about the wedding. It's about two people who are in love. Right now Rowan knows that Anne did not kill his mother. But how long do you think that will last if the evidence keeps piling up and no one comes to Anne's defense?" she sighed and closed her eyes for a moment before opening them again. "I can't even imagine Anne paying for a crime she didn't do, while Rowan spends the rest of his life believing that the woman he loved killed his own mother."

Brian shook his head with amazement as his gaze settled on her deep green eyes. "Most people would leave it to the courts to figure it out, Wendy. Most people would just move onto the next wedding. It amazes me how deeply you care for people."

Wendy pursed her lips slightly and lowered

her eyes. She knew that with Brian's experience with crime and the seedy side of life he probably thought of her as naive and foolish. She took a deep breath and lifted her eyes back to his.

"I don't know how people can go through life not caring, Brian," she said softly. "If we don't care about each other, what's the point?"

Brian offered a soft smile and nodded, "I think I am going to learn a lot from you, Wendy."

"Maybe just how to get yourself into the middle of things," Wendy said with a hint of despair. "Do you really think it's hopeless? There's nothing we can do to help Anne?"

"There's always something we can do," Brian said with determination. "If you're certain that Anne is not the killer, I believe you. I can't say that I'm as convinced as you, but I trust your instincts. So, let's figure out who else the killer could be. You told me about how Celeste treated you and Anne, but did she have any other enemies?"

"Enemies?" Wendy had to choke back a laugh. "I think it would be a shorter list to come up with people who were fond of her."

"Well, that is a good thing," Brian said with a half-smile and gave her hands a squeeze.

"How is that a good thing?" Wendy asked with confusion.

"It means that Anne wasn't the only one who hated her. That the more suspects we have, the better the chance that Anne can be exonerated." He swept his gaze over the gathering of family members, wedding party members, and staff from the hotel. Everyone was curious about the police presence. The rumor was spreading quickly through the hotel that a murder had been committed. With Anne being taken away, and Rowan beside himself, it was quite clear that someone important had been killed. Wendy's gaze settled on Chris who was pushing through the crowd to get to Rowan.

"Why was Anne being led out of here by the police?" he demanded as his gaze flicked from the police to Rowan. "Did she kill her? Did she kill our mother?" his voice was getting angrier by the moment.

"No!" Rowan shouted as an officer stepped between them. The brothers' voices were raising, and their anger was clearly reflected in their expressions.

"Then why has she been taken by the police?" Chris asked as he backed slightly away from the police officer.

"It's a mistake, it's all a mistake," Rowan insisted. "You know that, Chris. You know that Anne would never do this." Rowan looked desperately into his brother's eyes.

Chris nodded and turned away from Rowan for a moment before turning back. "You're right, I know she wouldn't. I just can't believe that this is happening."

"I was supposed to be getting married tomorrow," Rowan said, obviously bewildered. "Now what? Do we plan a funeral?"

"I don't know," Chris shook his head. "I don't know," he ran his hands back through his hair. Wendy pulled Brian aside.

"This is out of control, Brian," she said quickly. "I have to talk to Anne."

"Well, that's not possible, she is probably still being held at the station and being interviewed," Brian shook his head.

"Please Brian, I have to talk to her. I have to find out what happened, where exactly she went, who might have seen her. Brian, if I don't find out we can't do anything to protect her," Wendy spoke quickly and in a bit of a panic.

"Okay, okay, take a breath," Brian said soothingly and pulled her into a tight hug. "It's going to be okay, Wendy. We'll figure this out."

"How can it be?" Wendy asked in a whisper. "The groom's mother is dead, the bride is under arrest for her murder, how can any of this be okay?"

Brian raised an eyebrow and looked steadily into her eyes. "I have no doubt that you can make magic happen, Wendy, you do it all the time for people who are looking for a way to declare their love. Maybe there won't be a wedding, but there is still love to be declared, isn't there?"

Wendy stared at him with some shock. She had never heard him talk so romantically. "Yes, there is," she said quietly. "But Anne can't declare anything from a jail cell."

"All right," Brian nodded. "I'll see what I can do. I have a few favors I can call in," he hugged her a little closer and then released her. "Stick around here for a little while. I'll call you if I can arrange something."

"Thank you, Brian," Wendy said with some relief. "I'll see what I can find out here."

"Just be careful," Brian warned. "Be careful what you say, and how you say it. This place is going to be packed with not just police officers, but reporters, too. Until we figure out exactly what happened here, we need to be cautious."

"Okay, I'll be careful," Wendy promised him.

After Brian left the hotel, Wendy slipped into the lobby. She wanted to see exactly who the police had stopped to interview. It didn't take her long to spot the manager of the hotel being questioned by two police officers. Wendy positioned herself close enough to overhear what they were discussing.

"So, why was the room blocked off?" the first officer asked him.

"It was blocked off because there had to be repairs made to the walls, which then meant that it had to be painted," the manager explained.

"Who had access to the room on the hotel staff?" the other officer asked.

"Everyone," the manager shook his head. "I mean, the only people that should have been in there were the painters, but it wasn't locked up. Any of the staff members could have gone in at any time."

"The painters, can you give us their names?" the first officer asked.

"Of course I can, but it wasn't the painters. That's ridiculous. Obviously, this was someone with a personal vendetta," the manager shook his head.

"Maybe this would be easier if you came down to the station with us," the first officer suggested. "We can review the entire staff list and you can let us know who was working at the time, and whether any of your employees had direct conflicts with the victim."

"I guess, fine," the manager sighed. "I don't

understand why you're pursuing this, when you've already arrested the killer."

"Sir, we haven't arrested anyone, the investigation is still active," the second officer frowned. "We may have a suspect that we're questioning but that doesn't mean the case is closed."

Wendy felt a sense of relief at those words. To her, it meant she had time. She had time to discover the truth. She remembered the day before, when she had visited the security office. The security officer had explained that there were cameras all over the hotel. She was sure that the police had already collected the video from the security office, but she was hoping that it still might show something on it that she could use to defend Anne. She headed for the security office, doing her best to avoid the police officers along the way. As she neared the door, she spotted two officers standing a little further down the hall.

"I don't know," one of the police officers shook her head. "He said that there was some kind of problem with the cameras and he's trying to retrieve the data. He said it could take at least twenty minutes."

"Twenty minutes," the other officer frowned. "I hope he gets it done faster or Detective Dunn is going to take it out on me."

"I asked him to hurry," the first officer said quickly.

Wendy looked at the closed door to the security office. She was just deciding whether to knock or not when her cell phone rang. The officers both looked suspiciously in her direction. Wendy quickly pulled her phone out of her pocket and ducked around the corner. It was Brian. She quickly answered.

"Did you find out anything?" Wendy asked hurriedly in a hushed voice.

"They've already run the prints on the

murder weapon," Brian explained. "From the original results it's not good. There were only two sets. One belonged to Celeste and the other belonged to Anne."

"So?" Wendy frowned. "The knife belonged to Anne, it would be expected that her fingerprints are on it."

"Yes, it would," Brian agreed. "But it would also be expected that the murderer's fingerprints would be on the knife."

"Maybe the murderer wore gloves," Wendy suggested with a slight frown.

"If that were the case the fingerprints would likely be smudged. It's obvious that the knife was just polished, because of how few fingerprints are on it. It is most probable that the only two people to have touched it were Anne and Celeste. Clearly that only leaves one person who can be the murderer," he said with a sigh. "I'm sorry, Wendy, but they have more than enough to hold her on, and unless we can come up with another theory, there's not much chance that she's going to be released any time soon."

"Maybe, it's not so clear," Wendy said softly. "Maybe Celeste wasn't a victim at all, but took her own life."

"You think she stabbed herself in the chest?" Brian asked with disbelief in his voice. "There are much easier ways to take your own life."

"Maybe, but she was quite spiteful. Maybe she just wanted to make a scene, to draw attention, and didn't realize how much damage she had done until it was too late," Wendy suggested.

"If that were the case why did she do it tucked away in a room where no one would look for her? If she was hoping for some drama and some attention then wouldn't she have done it somewhere that she could be seen, or at least found easily, so she could get the medical help that she would need in order to survive the wound?"

Wendy sighed, deflated by his words. "I guess you're right about that," she said as she sighed again and looked at her hands. "I just don't think it's possible that Anne did this."

"It might not be possible," he agreed. "But right now, it's the only theory the police have."

"Can I see her?" Wendy asked.

"I'm still trying," Brian said and hung up the phone.

Wendy thought about the knife and the fingerprints trying to work out how they could only be Anne's and Celeste's. Maybe she was wrong and Anne was the killer. Just as that thought entered her mind her phone chimed. It was a text from Brian.

I've got you in to see her. Can you be here in 10?

On my way, she texted back as she hurried out into the parking lot trying not to draw attention to herself. She headed straight for her car.

Chapter Six

Wendy drove as quickly as she could to the police station. It was one of the last places she wanted to see again but she felt like she had no choice in the matter. She was on a mission. When she parked she glanced around nervously. She had some idea of how it must have felt for Anne to be swept into the police station, but this was a little different than what Wendy had experienced. Anne was facing losing her fiancé, and being convicted of his mother's death. She had to be absolutely terrified. She stepped inside the police station lobby where there were several rows of chairs set up. As soon as she was in the door, Brian stood up and grabbed her gently by the arm. He pulled her to the side of the lobby.

"I can get you in to see her," Brian said quietly and glanced over his shoulder to make sure that no one else was listening in. "But it has to be quick, and you can't say too much about the investigation, understand?"

"I do," Wendy nodded quickly and grasped the crook of his elbow. "Thank you, Brian. I'm sure she's losing her mind by now."

"Just keep your voice low, and act as if you belong here," Brian explained. "One of my buddies on the force is doing this favor for me, but if we get caught, he gets caught, and I don't want to get him into trouble or lose my police contacts."

"I will be quiet as a mouse," Wendy promised him. Brian nodded and led her down the short hallway towards the interrogation rooms. Wendy was a little uncomfortable when she saw them. It wasn't long ago that she was being questioned in one of them. Brian nodded to an officer that was standing at the end of the hall. The officer glanced up and down the hall, and then nodded to Brian and waved a little. Brian escorted Wendy to the officer, then he paused.

"I'll be right out here," he promised her. Wendy swallowed thickly. She had to resist asking him to stay with her. The idea of being alone in the belly of the police station was a little unnerving.

"Right in here," the officer said quietly. "You've got about three minutes."

Wendy nodded and whispered, "Thank you."

He opened the door to the small room. When Wendy stepped inside, she saw Anne resting her head on her arms, which were folded on top of the small, square table. She didn't even look up when Wendy walked over to the table.

"Anne," Wendy said gently, knowing that they didn't have a lot of time.

"Wendy?" Anne looked up with surprise. "What are you doing here?"

"I just want you to know that you have my support and I'm working on getting you out of here," Wendy said swiftly. "I want you to know that you're not alone, and I believe that you're innocent." They were the exact words that Wendy had needed to hear when she was being investigated as a murder suspect.

"What's the point?" Anne said morosely. "Rowan is never going to marry me now. The wedding is over. No one is going to believe that I had nothing to do with this. My life is over already."

"Anne, that's not true," Wendy insisted as she sat across from her. "Listen, I don't have a lot of time so I need you to be as honest as possible with me."

"Of course I will be," Anne nodded.

"You said you went for a walk after you and Celeste fought," Wendy reminded her. "I tried to call and text you during that time, did you have your cell phone?"

"No," Anne admitted. "I was so upset I just walked out. I left my phone, my purse, everything."

"Okay and where did you walk?" Wendy asked. "Down along the beach, or the grounds of the hotel?"

"I didn't want to go down to the beach, there were too many people who could have seen me crying," Anne gasped out. "Ironic isn't it, if I had let myself be seen I'd have an alibi?"

"Don't worry about that now, Anne," Wendy said sternly. "I need you to focus. Surely, someone would have seen you outside walking around the hotel. Or you must have seen someone. A maintenance man? Someone walking a dog? A wandering guest?"

"No, there was no one, I was crying too hard to notice," Anne blurted out.

"Anne, think about it," Wendy said grimly. "Even if you think that they didn't see you, did you notice anyone in the windows, walking around the garden, or near the pool?"

"Wait," Anne whispered. Wendy glanced at her watch. She only had about a minute left. "Chris!" she said suddenly. "I saw Chris. He was walking outside the hotel, right by the outside wall. I thought he was looking for me, and I didn't want to talk to him, or anyone. So, I turned and walked the other way before he could see me. How is that going to help?" she asked with a sigh.

"Don't worry, Anne, let me figure that out," Wendy said. "I have to go now, but I want you to know that I'm working to get you out of here. No matter what you believe, Rowan knows that you didn't kill his mother, Anne, he told the police that, too."

Anne sniffled and nodded. "That's good at least," she muttered. "Wendy," she whispered and lifted her eyes to the woman across from her.

"Yes?" Wendy asked, urgency surging through her veins.

"I didn't kill her. I really didn't, but," she lowered her voice. "I really wanted to."

Wendy stared at her for a brief moment, and then she nodded. "Just don't tell the police that, Anne," Wendy said calmly. She stood up and glanced towards the door. "I have to go. I will try to get you out of here as soon as I can."

"Okay," Anne sniffled. "Thank you. Can you check on my father please? He's staying at the hotel, I haven't been able to get hold of him. He didn't show up for the rehearsal lunch, and I'm very worried about him."

"I will," Wendy promised her before hurrying out the door. She closed it carefully behind her.

"What are you doing back here?" a sharp voice asked as Wendy stepped out of the interrogation room. She felt an icy blast course through her veins as she realized that she had been caught. Luckily, she had already closed the door behind her.

"I'm looking for the bathroom," she said as she turned towards the voice. Standing before her was a woman dressed from head to toe in a spotless business suit. She had stern, gray eyes and her dark brown hair was knotted at the base of her neck.

"Really?" she said with disbelief. "There are bathrooms in the lobby, there is no reason for you to be back here. What's your name?" she demanded. Wendy's heart was pounding. She knew that Brian had risked a lot by helping her out, and so had his friend. She didn't want him to lose his job over what had happened.

"Okay, you got me," Wendy said with a pout. "I'm not really looking for the bathroom."

"I know that, so what are you doing here and what is your name?" the woman demanded again as she took a step closer to Wendy.

"My name is Christina Johns," she explained quickly, and ignored the fact that she was lying to a person who was likely a police detective. "I'm a reporter, I just wanted to see if I could get the scoop on that murder that happened at the Sand Hotel. I heard it had something to do with a wedding, I just thought it would be an interesting piece."

"I could have you arrested, do you know that?" the woman snapped and searched Wendy's eyes with clear disapproval. "People's lives are not a game for you to play with."

"I know that," Wendy said softly as if she had been chastised. "I didn't mean to cause any trouble. I didn't even get any information. I slipped back here and I was just on my way back out."

"You better be telling me the truth," the woman said sharply. "I'm Paige Dunn, and I'm the detective working this case. If I see so much as a word about this case published under your name, I will have you arrested. Do you understand?"

Wendy nodded quickly. "I'm sorry," she said meekly.

"Officer," Detective Dunn snapped at a police officer that was walking by, the very same one that had allowed Wendy into the interrogation room. He looked at Detective Dunn guiltily. "Please escort this woman out of the building."

"Yes ma'am," the officer nodded and grabbed Wendy's arm rather roughly. He led her down the hall, right past Brian, and out the door into the parking lot. Wendy glanced over her shoulder to see Brian step out after her.

"That was too close," the officer said grimly. "I hope that you got something that you could use," he said with a shake of his head before he stepped back into the station.

"Did you?" Brian asked as he walked Wendy to her car.

"Maybe," Wendy replied. "I'm not sure yet."

"Well, what did she say?" Brian asked.

"She said she was out walking by herself, but she saw Chris out walking, too. She claims he didn't see her, but I think he might have," Wendy slid behind the steering wheel. Brian opened the passenger door and settled in beside her. Wendy glanced at him briefly with surprise.

"I told you I would help you," Brian said and reached out to give her hand a light pat. "We might as well carpool."

Wendy smiled a little at that and started the car. "Is that really all she said?" Brian asked with a frown. "It's not much to go on."

"It may not seem like much now," Wendy said with a slight nod. "But I think it's worth pursuing and it's all we've got. Before I can talk to Chris, I have to check on Anne's father. He wasn't at the lunch, and she hasn't been able to get hold of him."

"Hmm, absent at the time of the murder and now inaccessible?" Brian arched an eyebrow.

"He's very frail," Wendy said with a shake of her head.

"Don't do that," Brian warned. "Never dismiss a suspect just because of a snap judgment. There are plenty of people in the world that make themselves look weaker than they are. Never cross off a suspect unless you have proven their innocence."

"Guilty until proven innocent?" Wendy asked with a slight laugh.

"Yes," Brian replied in a serious tone. "The truth is everyone in that hotel today is a suspect. That means that Celeste's killer is still on the loose. You can't assume that you are safe with anyone."

"I guess you're right," Wendy nodded. "So, the sooner we find the murderer the better," she said with determination.

Chapter Seven

Wendy drove the rest of the way from the police station to the hotel in silence as she was processing what she had learned about the murder. Brian seemed to be doing the same as he stared out of the window. When Wendy pulled into the hotel parking lot she was more determined than ever to find the real murderer.

"I'm going to check on Arnold, then I want to see if there are copies of the video feed from the cameras around the hotel," she said to Brian as she pulled the key out of the ignition.

"Don't you think the police already have that?" Brian asked.

"I'm sure they do. But there is no harm in asking if there are any copies. I overheard that there was a problem with some of the footage. I want to find out what was actually retrieved. I want to see the feed from around the entire hotel

117

if possible. It's possible that Anne was caught somewhere else in the hotel or on the grounds around the time the murder was taking place."

"That's a good idea," Brian nodded. "It's amazing what cameras capture these days. But do you think you can get in to see the footage?"

"Yes, I think so. I met the security guard yesterday and he was very nice to me," Wendy explained as they walked into the lobby.

Wendy paused beside the front desk of the hotel. There was a clerk behind the desk, who looked a little overwhelmed.

"I need to know which room Arnold Max is staying in," Wendy said when the clerk finally looked up at her.

The clerk nodded and tapped on the keyboard for a moment before looking back at Wendy.

"He's staying in room 501," the clerk said softly. "Poor man."

"Why do you say that?" Wendy asked.

"Well, don't you know, it was his daughter that killed that poor woman," the clerk said with a slight gasp in her voice.

"I didn't know that," Wendy replied and narrowed her eyes. "It's not a good idea to gossip, especially when you aren't certain that something is true."

"Oh, sorry," the clerk blushed and lowered her eyes. Wendy and Brian walked to the elevator. There were still several police officers milling about, and Wendy spotted a few members from the wedding party scattered throughout the lobby and the banquet hall as well. Brian held the elevator doors so that Wendy could step in. Then he pressed the button for level five. As the elevator lurched and rose upward, Wendy glanced over at him.

"So much for keeping a lid on things, it looks like the rumor is spreading a lot faster than the investigation can move."

"That's going to make it harder on Anne," Brian said with a frown. "Public opinion can really have an impact on a trial. If she is seen as a murderer then that may influence how the court sees her as well."

"It just isn't right," Wendy said as she balled her hands into fists. "I don't think she's done anything wrong."

When they stepped off the elevator onto the fifth floor, the first room was the one they needed to go to. Wendy walked up to the door of the room and knocked lightly. There was no answer. She knocked a little harder. This time the door swung open as a result of her knocking. Wendy glanced over at Brian who shrugged slightly. Wendy nudged the door the rest of the way open.

"Arnold, are you in here?" she called out. "It's Wendy, your daughter's wedding planner."

Wendy heard a slight scuffling sound and glanced warily at Brian. Brian raised a hand and gestured for her to let him go in first. As he started to step in front of her, Arnold suddenly appeared at the door.

"I'm sorry, I didn't have my hearing aid in," he explained. "Wendy, right?" he asked as he settled his gaze on Wendy.

"Yes sir, your daughter Anne was concerned about you, and she asked me to check on you," Wendy explained.

"Concerned about me, why?" Arnold asked with surprise.

"She said she's been trying to reach you, but wasn't able to. Also, she was concerned because you didn't arrive on time for the rehearsal lunch," Wendy explained.

"Oh, nothing to worry about. I just wasn't feeling too well. I thought I'd stick to the room. I knew that if I told Anne that I wasn't feeling well, she would worry instead of enjoying the lunch. I want to make sure that I'm fresh for the wedding tomorrow," he added with a slight smile. Wendy and Brian exchanged a look.

"Sir, are you not aware of what happened here today?" Brian asked with a frown.

"I'm sorry, I'm not following," Arnold shook his head. "Have we met before?"

"No," Brian replied. "My name is Brian, I'm a friend of Wendy's," he said gently. "I am sorry to say but Celeste, Rowan's mother, was killed today in this hotel."

"What?" Arnold gasped.

"As of this moment, Anne is the main suspect," Brian said cautiously

"What?" Arnold asked again in shock. "Is this some kind of prank?" he demanded and looked at Wendy. "This is a cruel trick, there's nothing funny about this."

"I assure you, Sir, it's not a joke," Wendy

explained quickly. "I'm trying to help Anne. I know that she didn't do this. You're sure she didn't come to see you or text you earlier today?" she asked.

Arnold stared at her with blank, shocked eyes. "No," he muttered, and then shook his head. "No, this isn't right. This wasn't supposed to happen. I think I need to lie down now," he mumbled.

"Okay," Wendy nodded with understanding. "I know this is a lot to take in. I just want you to know that we are working towards clearing your daughter's name."

"Yes," he sighed and shook his head. Then he began walking back towards his bed.

"We should let him rest," Brian said quietly.

Wendy nodded and closed the door behind her. Once they were in the hall, Brian stopped her.

"You realize he has no alibi," he said calmly.

"Brian, he could barely stand up!" Wendy pointed out.

"Or, that's how he wanted it to seem."

Wendy was silent on the elevator ride down to the lobby. She knew that Brian's suspicions were founded but it was hard for her to think of a man as sweet and funny as Arnold as a suspect in such a terrible crime. Brian seemed oblivious to her silence as he followed behind her to the security room. There were no police officers in the hallway anymore, but the door to the security office was still closed. Wendy knocked lightly and then opened the door without waiting for an answer. The man inside was tapping lightly at his keyboard as he studied the monitor in front of him. He looked up swiftly when Wendy stepped in.

"I'm sorry to bother you," Wendy said quickly. "Do you remember me from yesterday?"

"Yes," he nodded and glanced past her at

Brian who was standing in the doorway.

"I know that it's been a crazy evening, but I was wondering if you could help me with something, Marcus," Wendy sat down in the chair beside him. "I'm Wendy by the way, and this is Brian."

"What can I help you with?" Marcus replied and again glanced awkwardly up at Brian. Brian was silent and stared right back at him.

"Well, I know that you probably already turned the footage from earlier over to the police, but I was wondering if you had any other cameras or angles. I'm looking for a way to prove that Anne is not the murderer," she explained.

"Oh well, that's simple enough," Marcus shrugged. He tapped the keyboard and a video began playing on the monitor in front of him. "Everything we have is stored on the computer. I gave the police lots of footage but this is a copy of some of the footage," he explained. "I think you'll find it's the most illuminating." Wendy watched the empty hallway for a few seconds. Then suddenly there was a woman walking down the hall. It wasn't Anne however, not with that sway or that smirk.

"That's Suzette," Wendy gasped, "the groom's sister-in-law."

"Exactly," Marcus nodded. "Now watch," he pointed to the door of the room where Celeste was killed. Sure enough, Suzette walked right up to it and opened the door. Once she had disappeared inside, the door closed.

"I can't believe this," Wendy shook her head. "I never thought that it would be her."

"Let's go find her," Brian said quickly.

"Thank you, Marcus, this has been a huge help," Wendy said with a warm smile.

"No problem," he replied.

As Wendy and Brian hurried out of the

security office, Brian leaned close to her.

"Are you sure you don't want to leave this to the police?" Brian questioned cautiously.

"I just want to see what Suzette has to say about it," Wendy said.

"She might have already been picked up by the police. If you want to speak to her we'll have to find her fast, that's even if she's still here," Brian explained. "I can't imagine why, if they've seen that video, she hasn't been arrested yet."

"They probably haven't had the copy long," Wendy explained. "Marcus was having some trouble getting the footage for them earlier. As for Suzette, I think I can make a pretty good guess as to where she might be. The hotel bar."

"Okay," Brian nodded. "Let's check it out."

Despite the chaos that had unfolded after the murder, the hotel bar was generally unaffected. There was a man playing the piano in the center of the room. There were several people lined up for drinks at the bar.

"There she is," Wendy said as she recognized Suzette. "Suzette," she called out as she walked up to her. Suzette turned with a mild frown.

"What is it?" she snapped.

"I need to talk with you for a moment," Wendy said. "It's very important. Can we step out into the hall?"

"Can I get my drink first?" Suzette asked with annoyance.

"I'm not serving you any more," the bartender said as she passed by the area where Suzette was leaning.

Suzette rolled her eyes. Then she followed Brian and Wendy out into the hall. Once in the hallway, Wendy turned to face Suzette.

"I think you need to tell the truth, Suzette," Wendy said calmly. "Before things get any more out of hand."

"The truth about what?" Suzette asked with annoyance.

"The truth about going into the room where your mother-in-law was murdered around the time of her murder," Brian said sternly. Suzette glared at him for a moment and then looked back at Wendy.

"Do you think I killed her?" Suzette gasped.

"Well, from the tape it looks like a possibility," Wendy stated diplomatically.

"Are you serious? I didn't kill the old bat. Why would I do that?" she shook her head.

"Maybe you were fed up?" Wendy suggested. "Or maybe you wanted Chris to get his inheritance faster. Whatever the reason, you need to make it clear that Anne had nothing to do with this crime."

"You're nuts," Suzette scowled. "I didn't kill Celeste."

"Suzette, we have you on camera going into

the very same room where Celeste was killed," Wendy said in a whisper. "How long do you think it's going to take the police to figure that out?"

"You're wrong," Suzette growled. "I had nothing to do with Celeste's death, though I can't say I blame Anne for finally snapping. It's always the sweet ones you know."

"No, I don't know," Wendy argued sternly. "I don't think Anne did this, and the footage we saw is proof of that."

"It can't be," Suzette frowned and took a step back. "I didn't do it, I wasn't there."

"Cameras don't lie," Brian pointed out gruffly.

"This time they do," Suzette insisted. She was starting to get irritated.

"Are you saying that wasn't you on the camera walking into the room?" Wendy asked incredulously.

"Okay look," Suzette sighed and shook her head. "I did go into the room. But it was earlier, and I wasn't in there with Celeste."

"So, you just picked a room that was being painted to hang out in?" Brian asked sharply. "Suzette, you've got to come up with something better than that."

"I just wanted a drink, in peace," Suzette explained with annoyance. "Having to put up with that woman is like nails scraping across a chalkboard. I needed a moment to myself, and I figured she wouldn't go near a room that was under renovation. So, I slipped in there to have a few drinks."

"And Celeste came in and caught you. Finally, you couldn't take her remarks anymore, so you snapped," Wendy supplied with confidence in her voice.

"No, no," Suzette shook her head quickly. "I didn't run into Celeste until I came out of the room. She was in the hallway. Looking for me of course. She made some terrible comments about smelling alcohol on my breath. I told her she was full of it, and I hadn't drunk a drop. She insisted that she was going to catch me in the act, and went into the room to find the bottle of alcohol."

"That probably made you angry enough to go in after her," Brian suggested and stepped a little closer to her. "So, maybe you followed her in."

"No," Suzette said firmly. "I went back to the banquet hall. I never went back in that room." Wendy and Brian exchanged glances. "Look, you don't have to believe me," Suzette continued. "But no matter what Celeste did to me, I wouldn't have killed her. She might have been a terrible mother-in-law, but Chris still loved her, and I would never hurt him like that."

She turned on her heel and stalked back into the bar.

Brian shifted closer to Wendy and spoke in a

whisper. "Do you believe her?" he asked.

"The question is do I believe her or do I believe a camera?" Wendy frowned. "Can cameras lie?"

"Not usually," Brian said with a shake of his head.

"Let's take another look at that video," Wendy said. "Maybe we missed something."

"Okay, it's worth another try," Brian agreed.

Chapter Eight

When Wendy and Brian got back to the security office the door was slightly open. Wendy pushed it open the rest of the way. There was no one inside. This struck her as odd, considering there had just been a murder, and potentially a killer on the loose. All of the monitors were on displaying live feed from the cameras, but no one was monitoring them.

"I think I can pull it up myself," Wendy said and started tapping at the keys.

"No, not like that," Brian warned and pulled her hands away from the keyboard. "Trust me, cameras I know."

Wendy stepped back and allowed Brian to sit down in front of the monitor. With a few quick keystrokes the video of Suzette walking into the room where Celeste was killed began playing.

Wendy leaned over his shoulder and

watched the video intently. As expected, Suzette emerged from the room and began walking down the hallway. The time stamp was shortly before Wendy had discovered the body. There was no hint of the video footage being tampered with. Wendy frowned.

"How is this possible?" she asked. "Suzette insists that she wasn't there at that time."

"She's obviously lying, Wendy. I know you like to give people the benefit of the doubt but I really think the video speaks for itself."

"Wait," Wendy leaned over his shoulder a little further and pointed at the monitor in front of them. "Look at that. Can you pause it?"

"Look at what?" he asked and tapped on the keyboard to pause the video.

"The clock," Wendy said as she pointed to the clock at the end of the hallway. "It has a different time than the timestamp on the video. The video says one thirty-five and the clock on the wall says about ten minutes past one."

Brian grunted quietly as he compared the two, then he nodded slowly. "You're right it does."

"So, what does that mean?" Wendy asked. She was getting more confused by the moment.

"Maybe the clock doesn't work," Brian suggested. "We should go check it out."

"Good idea," Wendy nodded. "The sooner the better. I can't even imagine what Anne is going through."

"Wendy, from what everyone has been saying about Celeste it sounds like she was giving Anne a really hard time. Don't you think it's possible she had something to do with this?" he asked as he stood up from the chair he had been sitting in.

"Did you see her on the video?" Wendy shot back impatiently. "How did she get in the room, if she's not on the video?"

Brian was silenced by her words. After a

moment he nodded. "Let's go check out that clock."

As the two slipped out of the security room, Wendy noticed Marcus hurrying down the hall towards the room, his thick, muscular frame walking as quickly as he could. She pulled Brian to the other side of the hallway before they could be spotted. As they were making their way towards the short hall that contained the room where Celeste was killed, voices drifting from an alcove near the banquet hall drew their attention.

"What do you mean they saw you on camera?" Chris asked heatedly.

Wendy pulled Brian back around the corner of the hallway so that they couldn't be seen.

"I don't know, they just said I'm on camera walking into the room and..."

"Unbelievable Suzette, seriously," he growled.

"What?" Suzette asked innocently. "You

know I had nothing to do with your mother's death, Chris. Is that what you're thinking?"

"No," he snapped back. "I'm thinking that if you hadn't been sneaking around drinking, maybe you wouldn't be in the crosshairs of a murder investigation right now."

"But it's not true," Suzette snapped.

"Do you think that really matters?" Chris argued in return. "Everyone knows you two were fighting. Everyone knows that you're a drunk. That's all that's going to matter to the police."

"I'm not a drunk," Suzette protested.

"Look Suzette, my mother might have been nuts, but she got one thing right. You aren't happy unless you have a drink in your hand, and even then you're pretty miserable," he shot back with frustration.

"Maybe I wouldn't be if you had stood up for me once in a while, Chris," she replied tearfully. "Even Rowan tries to stand up for Anne. But you,

you never said a word."

"You don't know that," he hissed in return. "You have no idea what I've done for you, Suzette."

Wendy glanced over at Brian as she heard those words.

"Do you think he might have?" she whispered.

Brian put his finger lightly to his lips. Footsteps were approaching from the hallway. Wendy was sure they would be caught spying. Brian must have thought the same thing, because he suddenly pulled her into his arms, and pressed her back against the wall. He kissed her heavily as Suzette and Chris walked past them, still squabbling.

"I want you to tell me what you mean," Suzette was demanding.

"We'll talk about it later," Chris hissed and hurried her down the hallway.

Wendy barely heard them, she was too busy kissing Brian right back and getting lost in the warm glow that flowed through her from head to toe. When Brian finally broke the kiss he gazed into her eyes for a long moment. Wendy reveled in the intimacy of him being so close. But they both knew that there was a lot at stake at the moment.

"Did you hear the way Chris talked?" Wendy asked.

Brian's lips tensed for a moment, and Wendy realized that it might not have been the right moment to start talking about the case again.

"Yes, I heard him," Brian nodded as he took a slight step back. "Let's check out that clock, and then I think we need to talk to Chris."

They continued down the hall and then turned down the short hall in the direction of the room where the murder had been committed. They walked to the end and paused in front of the clock at the end of the hallway. The second hand was sweeping as it should have been.

"It's accurate," Brian said as he compared the time on the clock to the time on his watch.

"But how can it be?" Wendy asked with confusion.

"I'm not sure," Brian admitted. "Let's talk to Chris, and then we can check with maintenance to see if anyone replaced or repaired the clock between the time of the murder and now."

"Good idea," Wendy agreed. They didn't have to go far to find Chris. As soon as they stepped out of the short hallway they found him walking towards the lobby, alone.

"Chris," Wendy called out. "I need to speak with you."

"Not now, Wendy," Chris said and started to brush past her.

"Wait a minute, Chris," Brian said and placed his hand firmly on Chris' chest. "We just have a few questions for you. Wendy just needs a minute."

Chris narrowed his eyes and glanced from Brian to Wendy, then back to Brian again. "What is this about?" he shrugged. "Neither of you is the police, I don't have to answer your questions."

"I think it's in your best interests to answer them," Brian said sternly.

"Listen," Wendy said quickly before things could escalate. "You're right, Chris, we're not the police. You don't have to answer our questions. But I think you know that Anne is innocent of this crime. Do you really want her to be locked away for the rest of her life for something she didn't do?"

Chris pushed Brian's hand away from his chest and turned towards Wendy.

"That's for the police to figure out, isn't it?" he said grimly.

"So far they have every reason to believe that Anne did this. But I think that you know something that could clear her name, don't you?" Wendy asked and locked eyes with Chris.

Chris frowned and glanced away from her. "I don't know what you're talking about," he said gruffly.

"Yes, I think you do," she replied and took a step closer to him. She did her best to put together a confident expression. She had no idea if it was effective or not. "I think you saw Anne when she was walking around outside, but you don't want to admit it. You know that she couldn't have killed your mother, because you saw her with your own eyes. So, what are you trying to hide, Chris? Are you the one that couldn't take a minute more of your mother's behavior?"

"Wendy," Brian warned, as his eyes widened. Wendy hadn't intended to accuse Chris of murdering his own mother, but once she got moving she had a hard time slowing down.

"No!" Chris nearly shouted. Then he glanced around quickly and lowered his voice. "Look my mother was never a peach, but she was still my mother. I wouldn't kill her," he said with exasperation. "That's not why."

"Then why?" Brian pressed. "Do you have something against Anne? Are you hoping she takes the fall?"

"No," Chris sighed. "Anne is a nice person. I don't know how my brother got lucky enough to snag her. She doesn't deserve any of this."

"So, help her," Wendy asked desperately as she looked into Chris' eyes. "This isn't fair, she tried her hardest to be kind and loving to your mother and your entire family. How do you think her father is taking all of this?"

Chris cringed and ran a hand across his face. He seemed to be biting his lip in an attempt to keep from saying something.

"All right, the truth is, I was looking for someone," he said gravely. "I didn't want to come forward about it, because I don't want to cast any more suspicion on her."

"Who were you looking for?" Wendy asked.

"It was Suzette, wasn't it?" Brian suggested as he looked directly at Chris. "You went looking for your wife."

"Yes," he sighed. "I saw her disappear down a hallway, but I didn't want her to think I was following her. I just wanted to make sure she was safe. She had already been drinking, and," he frowned, "it's been an issue, especially when my mother was around. When I peeked in the window and saw her knocking back a few drinks in the room by herself, I decided to leave her alone and let her have some peace. As I was walking back around the hotel, I saw Anne. She was upset, and I knew that she would tell Suzette that she had seen me. Then Suzette would know I had been following her. So, I just walked the other way," he ran his hand back through his short, brown hair. "I didn't mean to get her into trouble," he said as he lowered his eyes.

"What do you mean?" Brian said.

"Before I knew what was happening I told the police that I saw someone in the room where Celeste was murdered," he said in a whisper. "Once I realized what I had said I told them that I thought it was Anne," Chris confided.

"You were the one that told the police you saw her going into the room," Wendy said as everything started falling into place.

"I didn't mean to get her into trouble," Chris said apologetically. "I just couldn't tell them I had seen Suzette."

"But once you knew what had happened, and that Anne was being accused you should have said something," Wendy admonished with a scowl.

"I should have," he agreed, his jaw muscles clenching tightly. "But how could I tell the police that I had seen my own wife in the very room where my mother was killed? How could I place her in that position of suspicion?"

"You were trying to protect her," Brian supplied.

"Of course I was, I love my wife," he sighed. "We have our problems. My mother was not the most affectionate person, so Rowan and I, we're a little lost when it comes to relationships. But Suzette is a good woman. She has a problem with drinking, but she's never hurt anyone because of it. She doesn't drink and drive or anything like that. How could I tell the police that my drunk wife who hated my mother was holed up drinking in the very room where my mother was killed? Who was going to believe that she didn't commit the murder?" he demanded.

Wendy looked over at Brian. Brian was still staring hard at Chris, assessing whether he believed the man's story or not. Wendy didn't have to stare at him. She did believe him. But there was one problem. Even if the video was tampered with and they could prove it, there was still plenty of evidence that Suzette had motive and opportunity, and her judgment was obviously impaired. She was as good, if not a better suspect than Anne. There was no way Chris was going to come forward to give Anne an alibi, if it meant incriminating his wife more than she already had been.

"Look," Chris sighed and shook his head. "I know that Anne didn't do this. Hell, it could have been anyone at the lunch. It could have been anyone who worked at the hotel. My mother did not exactly make friends easily. Honestly, I really thought Suzette had done it at first. But she told me she didn't, and I believe her."

"So do I," Wendy said softly.

"You do?" both Chris and Brian asked with surprise.

"Yes," Wendy said as she looked at Brian. "Suzette had plenty of opportunity to lose it with Celeste prior to today. Why would anything Celeste had done push her over the edge today? It's nothing she wasn't used to. Besides, we believe that the video might have been tampered with. I don't think Suzette would tamper with it to frame herself for murder, do you?"

Brian nodded slowly and rubbed his chin. "The only problem is, the police aren't going to find that good enough. And I think you need to accept that with the fingerprint evidence Anne is probably their best suspect."

"Unless we figure out who actually committed the murder both Anne and Suzette are going to remain under suspicion," Wendy glanced over at Chris for a moment. "You said that you saw Suzette in the room by herself. Did you see Celeste in there or at any time while you were walking around the hotel?"

"No," Chris shook his head. "I had no idea

she had even gone into that room until her body was found. Like I said I just peeked in the window. Now, I really have to go," he turned and hurried off down the hallway, leaving Brian and Wendy to consider what he had said.

"Maybe Chris did see his mother," Wendy suggested. "Maybe he saw the way she talked to Suzette in the hallway. Maybe he decided to take the chance to finally end it all and slipped inside the room after Suzette left."

"But he had to know that would put Suzette at risk," Brian shook his head. "He loves his wife."

"So he says," Wendy pointed out. "Divorce is very expensive, especially for the wealthy, Brian. Maybe he saw it as an opportunity to get out of a souring marriage without having to worry about alimony or a divorce settlement. No one is going to expect him to share his estate with someone who killed his mother."

"Wow, Wendy," Brian shook his head. "I never even thought of it that way."

"Look, I don't believe that Anne did this, and now we know that Chris saw her walking around the hotel at the time the murder took place. I don't think that Suzette did this either, she was too drunk not to be sloppy. Besides that, she wouldn't frame herself by doctoring the video. Chris had the motive, the means, and the opportunity," she nodded.

"But how would he get to the recording to change it?" Brian asked with a shake of his head. "I mean, he'd have to have access to it."

"Money talks," Wendy shrugged. "Maybe we should have another talk with the security guard before we speak to maintenance about the clock. But first, I want to find Rowan."

"Rowan?" Brian asked. "Why?"

"Call it a hunch but I don't think Chris did this alone," Wendy said grimly. "If he is the killer, I bet

Rowan did whatever he could to help protect his brother."

Chapter Nine

Brian and Wendy did not have to look far to find Rowan. When they stepped into the lobby there was a gathering of reporters near the front door. Rowan was standing right in the middle of them. Wendy was more than a little surprised. She hadn't expected Rowan of all people to want media attention so swiftly.

"Unfortunately, due to the circumstances of the investigation I can't offer any further information," Rowan was speaking in an even tone to the reporters. "I just want to say that my mother was a good woman, she didn't deserve this. Whoever committed this crime should pay dearly for what they have done."

"Isn't it true that your fiancée is the prime suspect and is down at the police station now?" one of the reporters asked.

"There was a bit of chaos after the body was

discovered, mistakes have been made," Rowan replied. "My fiancée had nothing to do with this, and her name will be cleared with time. Please understand that this is a time of grief for my entire family, including my fiancée, and that we ask for privacy."

Wendy rolled her eyes and glanced over at Brian. "Why would he call a press conference to ask for privacy?"

"I don't know, but I can tell you that Detective Dunn is not going to be happy about it," Brian replied. "There's no way she would approve of Rowan going to the media so soon."

As the reporters dispersed Rowan began to walk across the lobby. Brian and Wendy walked over to him.

"Rowan," Wendy said gently. "How are you doing?"

"As well as I can be, I suppose," Rowan replied with a frown. "I've heard from my brother,

Chris, that now the police are investigating his wife," he shook his head slightly. "They're wasting all of this time investigating two obviously innocent women, while the actual killer is free to escape."

"So, you don't suspect Suzette?" Brian asked. Rowan eyed him for a long moment and then shook his head.

"Suzette wouldn't do that. She may be a drunk, but she's never done anything worse than break a glass. What they should be doing is investigating the staff around here. Obviously, this was an inside job. Why else would my mother have ever gone near a room like that?" he shook his head. "She wouldn't have been able to stand such a messy environment."

"So, you think it was a staff member?" Wendy asked. "But why would anyone employed at the hotel do such a thing?"

"I don't know," Rowan shrugged. "Does it

matter? All that really matters is that she's gone. Nothing can change that. Especially not a wild goose chase."

"And where were you, Rowan?" Brian asked as he studied the man intently.

"Me?" Rowan replied with wide, innocent eyes. "Are you asking me where I was when my mother was killed?" he demanded as he glared at Brian.

"We're just trying to figure out the best way to help Anne," Wendy interjected. "I believe, as you do, that she had nothing to do with this murder. The more we know about the location of everyone at the time of Celeste's death, the better the chance that we can find something to clear her name."

"So, you think treating me like a suspect will help with that?" Rowan asked, his lip curled into a sneer.

"I am just trying to get an idea of what was

happening during the murder," Wendy replied with confidence. "If you really love Anne, as you claim you do, you will answer any question necessary to help her out of this situation." Rowan stared at her for a long moment, and then finally nodded.

"I was looking for Anne," Rowan replied with a sigh. "After my mother took off with the knife, I tried to comfort Anne, but she was inconsolable. Chris and I went to see if we could find our mother, but we got separated while we were looking through the hotel. I decided to go back to Anne to try to assure her that we could still have the wedding, but when I got back she was gone. So was Suzette. I thought maybe they were together. So, I went searching through the hotel for the two of them. I ran into the manager at the front desk. He said he hadn't seen Anne. By the time I headed back towards the banquet room, the police were already arriving. I didn't know what was going on," he admitted. "If something I said or did can help Anne, then please, use it."

Wendy shook her head slightly. "I'm not sure if it can but we will do our best, Rowan."

"Thank you," he said quietly. As Rowan walked across the lobby Brian scratched at his cheek slowly.

"It seems to me that we have a problem," he sighed.

"What's that?" Wendy asked as she looked over at him.

"Well, we've been doing our best to prove Anne's innocence, but all we've managed to do is prove that just about everyone who knew or was related to Celeste is potentially guilty, which is a good thing," he met Wendy's eyes. "But, I'm not so sure we're quickly going to be able to figure out who the actual killer is."

"Don't say that," Wendy said sternly. "You're an amazing investigator, Brian, and I'm, well, I'm just too stubborn to let this go. We're going to get to the bottom of it. I think the first thing we need to do is talk to Marcus. I want to get his opinion on whether the recording could have been tampered with."

"Okay," Brian agreed. They headed back to the security office. Marcus was sitting in his chair, studying the cameras in front of him.

"Hi again, Marcus," Wendy said as she stepped inside the room.

"Oh hi," Marcus said as he glanced up at her. Wendy noticed that the camera on the main monitor in front of Marcus was the camera that was recording the activities in the lobby. Wendy felt a little uneasy knowing that Marcus might have just been watching them.

"Can I pick your brain about something?" Wendy asked.

"Sure," he nodded as he turned his brawny frame to look at her. "What is it?"

"I was wondering, is there any way to tamper

with the footage once it's recorded?" she asked.

"I'm sorry, I wouldn't know anything about that," Marcus replied quickly.

"So, you have no idea how to change the timestamp on a recording?" Brian asked as he stepped up behind Marcus' chair. "Not even if someone paid you quite a bit to do it?"

"Excuse me?" Marcus said sharply. "That would be illegal and immoral," he turned and glared over his shoulder at Brian.

"I'm sorry, Marcus, we're not accusing you," Wendy said quickly. "It's just that we noticed the time on the clock in the recording was different to the timestamp."

"So?" Marcus shrugged. "The clock is probably broken."

"It isn't," Brian said sternly. "We checked."

"Well," Marcus frowned. "Why don't you check with Darren, he's in charge of maintenance for that wing of the hotel? Maybe he replaced the clock."

"I'll go check with him now," Wendy nodded.

"I'll stay here," Brian said calmly. "I'd like to see that video one more time."

"I don't know," Marcus hesitated. "I really shouldn't be letting you see any of this."

"Maybe not, but you already did," Brian pointed out. "We're not trying to make any trouble for you, Marcus. We just want to help Anne."

"Right," Marcus nodded. "But just one more time."

As Wendy walked out of the security office to find Darren, Marcus began playing the video again for Brian. Wendy headed for the lobby where the same clerk was still behind the desk.

"Can I speak with the manager?" Wendy asked.

"I'm sorry he's still dealing with the police,"

the clerk replied. "Is there something I can help you with?"

"I hope so," Wendy replied. "I'd like to speak to Darren, he's a maintenance worker."

"Darren," the woman repeated slowly. "There's no Darren that works in maintenance."

"Are you sure?" Wendy asked with confusion. "Marcus from security just told me that I should speak with Darren from maintenance."

"I'm sure," the clerk replied with narrowed eyes. "I know everyone that works in maintenance and there is no Darren. Marcus is fairly new anyway, I'd doubt he even knows who works in maintenance."

"Oh, I didn't realize he was new," Wendy frowned. "Maybe he just got the name confused then. I'm just trying to find out if a clock in one of the hallways had been repaired or replaced."

"Oh, I can check on that," the clerk said. "We

keep a record of all items that are in need of repair or replacement. It's a pretty big database, but I can search it by item."

"Can you narrow it down by date, too?" Wendy asked. "This clock would have been replaced today between about one and this evening."

"I doubt it," the clerk said quietly. "Maintenance only works part time so they usually only work until midday, after that they only do emergency calls. Oh, here we go," she shook her head slowly as she looked at the screen. "No repairs or replacements on clocks, not just today but not even in the whole week."

"Thank you," Wendy said with a slight frown.

Was it possible someone had replaced the clock without documenting it? Wendy couldn't think of a single reason why. As she walked back to the security office, her mind was working slowly through everything that Marcus had said.

He seemed to be certain about the name Darren. He also hadn't mentioned anything about being new. She recalled his comment to her, about watching over her. Her stomach churned slightly. If the clock hadn't been replaced, the only explanation possible was that the video had definitely been tampered with. It looked like the only person who seemed to have had the opportunity to do that was Marcus. If no one had paid him to do it, why would he do it? What would he get out of making it look as if Suzette had killed Celeste? It didn't make much sense to her.

Then all of a sudden the pieces slowly began to fit into place. Marcus tampered with the tapes for his own benefit. And the reason he would do that was if he was covering for someone else. Or if he was the murderer himself. He had access to the cameras. Which meant he could have altered them if he wanted to. The only reason she could think why he would want to, was to protect himself, or somebody else. He had delayed giving the tapes to the police, claiming there was a problem with retrieving them. He had plenty of time to tamper with the recording.

He probably lied about a Darren working in maintenance to get her and Brian out of the office. But Brian was still in the office. Her heartbeat quickened as she hastened her pace towards the security office. The only thing she couldn't work out was who Marcus would protect and if he was protecting himself why would he want to murder Celeste.

By the time Wendy reached the door of the security room, her heart was pounding heavily. She took a deep breath before she opened the door, she wasn't sure how she was going to get Marcus to admit the truth without putting herself and Brian in danger. Hopefully she wasn't too late and Brian wasn't already in danger.

Chapter Ten

When Wendy opened the door to the room she had horrible visions of finding Brian hurt and in trouble but she sighed with relief to find Brian and Marcus standing next to each other looking at the recordings. She immediately started doubting her theories. Maybe Marcus had nothing to do with the murder.

All of a sudden Marcus turned and pushed his full bodyweight towards Brian, Brian reached into his pocket to get his gun, but the full force from Marcus knocked the gun out of Brian's hand and the wind out of Brian.

Before Wendy could react Marcus wrapped his beefy arm around Brian's neck and started squeezing. Brian's fingers started digging and swiping at Marcus' arm but to no avail. Wendy was in shock as she saw the flush in Brian's cheeks and realized that he was really struggling to breath. Marcus locked eyes with Wendy and growled.

"You shouldn't have come back here."

His voice jolted Wendy out of the state of shock she had been lost in. She rummaged in her purse for a weapon. When her fingers struck the smooth surface of the cake-cutting knife she had tucked away there earlier, her heart skipped a beat. She whipped it out of her purse and lunged forward at Marcus and Brian. Never in her life had Wendy imagined that she would have cause to stab someone, but seeing Brian's body growing weaker in Marcus' grasp gave her the reason. She lodged the blade deep into the arm that was wrapped around Brian's neck. Marcus yelped and gasped at the same time resulting in a disturbing choking sound. He released Brian as he grimaced in pain. The blood flowing from the wound that Wendy had caused was beginning to drip on the floor.

"Brian, are you okay?" Wendy asked

fearfully.

"My gun," Brian managed to force his words out.

Wendy suddenly realized that she had made a grave mistake by leaving the knife wedged in Marcus' arm. He could easily pull it out and use it against them. Wendy looked around on the floor until she found the gun that Brian had lost in his struggle with Marcus. She snatched it up from the floor and handed it to Brian just as quickly. Brian pointed the weapon at Marcus.

"Don't move," he warned the man.

Wendy could see a deep purple bruise already forming on Brian's neck. The sight of it was quite scary. She realized just how close she had come to losing him. She pulled out her phone to call for help. Marcus sat down hard on the floor. Tears were bubbling up and spilling over his thick, dark lashes, both from pain and from being caught.

"I wasn't going to kill you," he stammered out. "I didn't mean to kill anybody."

"Oh, you weren't going to kill me?" Brian shot back. "Because not being able to breathe usually leads to death." Brian turned to Wendy. "When you walked in I had just asked him why there was a small skip in the video," he explained. "And well, you saw what happened next," he added with a hint of embarrassment.

"Sometimes, I just lose my temper," Marcus admitted darkly.

"Is that what happened to Celeste?" Wendy asked. "It was you that changed the time on the security video. Did she say or do something to make you lose your temper?"

"I'm a nice guy, most of the time," Marcus complained. He had his hand cupped around the knife that he was afraid to pull out of his arm. "But that woman was a terrible person. I saw the way she was treating everyone"

"So you killed her?" Brian asked with a hint of disbelief.

"The way she treated my sister pushed me over the edge." Marcus admitted as he shook his head.

"Your sister?" Wendy questioned.

"She was just trying to run a business, and take care of her child, she didn't deserve to be treated like that!" he exclaimed. "I saw everything on the camera, and she was so upset when she told me about it. I just couldn't believe that a person could be so cruel."

"Your sister?" Wendy repeated.

"Lisa," Marcus explained.

Wendy's eyes widened. "Lisa the florist?" she asked.

"Yes," Marcus nodded. "She's the one that got me the job here. I felt like I owed her. So, I just went to talk to Celeste. I was just going to explain that my sister deserved the job and that she shouldn't treat people that way," he said with sadness.

"What happened then?" Wendy coaxed him.

"She called me a loser, said I was worthless and so was my sister. I got angry," he lowered his eyes. "I'm not proud of it, but I pushed that old woman, hard."

"Don't you mean you stabbed her?" Brian interjected with a shake of his head.

"No, I didn't," Marcus insisted. "At least, I didn't mean to. When I pushed her, she slipped on the plastic that the painters had left down. She lost her balance. She fell on her purse," he murmured.

"The knife must have fallen out of her purse and wedged into her chest," Wendy gasped as she realized that was why the murder weapon only had two sets of fingerprints.

"It did," Marcus grimaced. "I turned her over, I thought maybe I could help her, but she was already gone. It wasn't really my fault though, was it?" he asked with fresh tears in his eyes. "I didn't mean to kill her. I didn't mean it."

"But you did," Wendy said with a frown.

"And you tried to kill me," Brian reminded Marcus. "You have a lot to answer for."

"Why did you try to frame Suzette?" Wendy asked. "Especially seeing as Anne had been arrested."

"I didn't have anything against the woman," Marcus sighed. "After what happened I knew that I would be on camera. I couldn't just erase it, because that would leave the time of the murder wiped clean, and that would point right to me. So, I reviewed the tape from earlier, I saw Suzette going into the room. I just changed things around so that it looked as if she had gone into the room around the time Celeste was killed. I never even thought about the clock," he grimaced.

"Marcus," Wendy shook her head. "You killed a woman, and you nearly destroyed two lives after the fact."

Marcus hung his head and gasped in pain. "I didn't mean any of it," he mumbled. Brian stepped close to Wendy and grasped her hand gently. He met her eyes.

"It looks like Anne will be able to come home tonight after all."

Wendy nodded. She felt some relief, but not entirely. Marcus, a man whose initial intention was to protect his sister, was going to be in jail for a long time. The wedding certainly couldn't go on after Celeste's death, at least not right away. There was a lot to be grateful for, with Anne's name cleared, but she just hoped that everything else would work out.

Wendy stepped aside as police officers arrived along with EMTs. Brian and Wendy were practically pushed out of the small room.

Detective Dunn hurried down the hallway. She stopped short when she saw Wendy standing close to Brian.

"The reporter?" she asked with a furrowed brow. "You're the one who figured this out?"

"I'm not exactly a reporter," Wendy replied softly.

"Then what are you?" Detective Dunn asked with confusion.

"I'm a wedding planner," Wendy replied and rested her head lightly against Brian's shoulder.

"You must take your job very seriously," Detective Dunn said with a small shake of her head. "I'll keep that in mind when I set a date."

Wendy reached into her purse and handed Detective Dunn a business card. "Wendy the wedding planner at your service," she said with an exhausted smile. "I have a feeling you're going to want to talk to me anyway."

"I'll be in touch," Detective Dunn nodded and

continued on to the security office.

Once they were alone in the hallway again Brian pulled Wendy into his arms.

"Are you okay?" he asked her in a whisper.

"You're the one who was nearly choked to death, and you're asking me?" she sputtered out and avoided his eyes.

"You're the one who saved my life, and stabbed someone to do it," Brian reminded her. He caught her chin lightly with his fingertips and turned her face back towards his. "I know that wasn't easy."

"I didn't think it would bother me so much," she whispered as she met his eyes.

"You did what you had to do, and I thank you for that," he smiled slightly.

"I think you should get checked out," Wendy said as she nodded towards the bruise across the front of his neck.

"I will," he replied and rested his head briefly on the top of hers. "I'm just not ready to let go of you yet."

Wendy smiled against his shoulder and wrapped her arms around him. She held him gently against her. In that moment with police officers and hotel security running up and down the hallway, it seemed to Wendy that their surroundings ceased to exist. There was only the warmth they shared between them.

There might not be a wedding the next day, but Wendy knew that Anne and Rowan would have the opportunity to declare their love when they were ready. She was only glad that she could be a part of making sure that they had the chance.

"Don't forget you owe me dinner," Brian whispered beside her ear.

"That is something I have no intention of forgetting," Wendy smiled and kissed him softly.

More Cozy Mysteries by Cindy Bell

Dune House Cozy Mystery Series

Seaside Secrets

Heavenly Highland Inn Cozy Mystery Series

Murdering the Roses

Dead in the Daisies

Killing the Carnations

Drowning the Daffodils

Suffocating the Sunflowers

Bekki the Beautician Cozy Mystery Series

CPSIA information can be obtained
at www.ICGtesting.com
Printed in the USA
LVHW081822170120
644014LV00033B/1043